International Praise for

I HAVE THE RIGHT TO DESTROY MYSELF

"[Kim's] novels are fragments of his amazing imagination. With uncommon creativity, grotesque images, and stories that build on and into each other like a computer game, he perplexes his readers as much as he delights them."

—*Leaders Korea* literary magazine

"A crime aesthete. With joyful cynicism, [Kim] offers a first novel about Love and Death in Seoul."   —*Le Monde* (France)

"Published in Korea in 1996, this was Kim's first novel. For critics and the public alike, this has been an exhilarating hit, and the young man—only 28—is clearly the leader of a new literary generation in his country. Manipulative and twisted, with as much grace as his narrator, the young writer has ... made a book about Eros and Thanatos, Seoul-style circa the 90s."

—*Lire* (France)

"With this book, Kim has become a Korean literary cult figure."

—*Spiegel Spezial* (Germany)

"Cool, urban, and very clever." —*Süddeutsche Zeitung* (Germany)

"Fast-paced, comic, slick, and heavily under American influence."

—*Der Tagesspiegel*

I HAVE THE RIGHT
TO DESTROY MYSELF

I HAVE THE RIGHT
TO DESTROY MYSELF

YOUNG-HA KIM

TRANSLATED FROM THE KOREAN BY
CHI-YOUNG KIM

A HARVEST ORIGINAL
HARCOURT, INC.
ORLANDO   AUSTIN   NEW YORK   SAN DIEGO   TORONTO   LONDON

Requests for permission to make copies of
any part of the work should be submitted online at
www.harcourt.com/contact or mailed to the following address:
Permissions Department, Harcourt, Inc.,
6277 Sea Harbor Drive, Orlando, Florida 32887-6777.

www.HarcourtBooks.com

The English version of the text by Tristan Tzara on page 47 originally
appeared in *The Dada Painters and Poets,* edited by Robert Motherwell;
copyright © 1951 by Wittenborn, Schultz, Inc. Reproduction of the text
in this book courtesy of Wittenborn Art Books: www.art-books.com.

This is a translation of *Naneun nareul pagoehal gwolliga itta,*
first published by Munhakdongne Publishing Company in 1996.

Library of Congress Cataloging-in-Publication Data
Kim, Young-ha, 1968–
[Na nun na rul p'agoehal kwolli ka itta. English]
I have the right to destroy myself/Young-ha Kim
translated from the Korean by Chi-Young Kim.
p. cm.
1. Kim, Young-ha, 1968– —Translations into English.
I. Kim, Chi-Young. II. Title.
PL992.415.Y5863N313 2007
895.7'34—dc22 2006031751
ISBN 978-0-15-603080-9

Text set in Sabon

Printed in the United States of America
First U.S. edition
C E G I K J H F D B

I HAVE THE RIGHT
TO DESTROY MYSELF

PART I
THE DEATH OF MARAT

I'M LOOKING AT JACQUES-LOUIS

David's 1793 oil painting, *The Death of Marat*, printed in an art book. The Jacobin revolutionary Jean-Paul Marat lies murdered in his bath. His head is wrapped in a towel, like a turban, and his hand, draped alongside the tub, holds a pen. Marat has expired—bloodied—nestled between the colors of white and green. The work exudes calm and quiet. You can almost hear a requiem. The fatal knife lies abandoned at the bottom of the canvas.

I've already tried to make a copy of this painting several times. The most difficult part is Marat's expression; he always comes out looking too sedate. In David's Marat, you can see neither the dejection of a young revolutionary in the wake of a sudden attack nor the relief of a man who has escaped life's suffering. His Marat is peaceful but pained, filled with hatred but also with understanding. Through a dead man's expression David manages to realize all of our conflicting innermost emotions. Seeing this painting for the first time, your eyes initially rest on Marat's face. But his face doesn't tell you anything, so your gaze moves in one of two directions: either toward the hand clutching the letter or the hand hanging limply outside of the tub. Even in death, he has kept hold of the letter and the pen. Marat was killed by a woman who had written him earlier, as he was drafting a reply to her letter. The pen Marat grips into death injects tension into the calm and serenity of the scene. We should all emulate David. An artist's passion shouldn't create passion. An artist's supreme virtue is to be detached and cold.

Marat's assassin, Charlotte Corday, lost her life at the guillotine. A young Girondin, Corday decided that Marat must be eliminated. It was July 13, 1793; she was twenty-five years old. Arrested immediately after the incident, Corday was beheaded four days later, on July 17.

Robespierre's reign of terror was set in motion after Marat's death. David understood the Jacobins' aesthetic imperative: A revolution cannot progress without the fuel of terror. With time that relationship inverts: The revolution presses forward for the sake of terror. Like an artist, the man creating terror should be detached, cold-blooded. He must keep in mind that the energy of the terror he releases can consume him. Robespierre died at the guillotine.

I close my art book, get up, and take a bath. I always wash meticulously on the days I work. After my bath, I shave carefully and go to the library, where I look for clients and scan through potentially helpful materials. This is slow, dull work, but I plod through it. Sometimes I don't have a single client for months. But I can survive for half a year if I find just one, so I don't mind putting long hours into research.

Usually I read history books or travel guides at the library. A single city contains tens of thousands of lives and hundreds of years of history, as well as the evidence of their interweaving. In travel guides, all of this is compressed into several lines. For example, an introduction to Paris starts like this:

> Far from just a secular place, Paris is the holy land of re-
> ligious, political, and artistic freedom, alternately bran-
> dishing that freedom and secretly yearning for more of
> it. Known for its spirit of tolerance, this city has been
> the refuge for thinkers, artists, and revolutionaries like
> Robespierre, Curie, Wilde, Sartre, Picasso, Ho Chi Minh,
> and Khomeini, along with many other unusual figures.
> Paris has fine examples of excellent 19th-century urban
> planning, and like its music, art, and theater, its archi-
> tecture encompasses everything from the Middle Ages
> to the avant-garde, sometimes even beyond the avant-
> garde. With its history, innovations, culture, and civi-
> lization, Paris is a necessity in the world: If Paris did not
> exist, we would have to invent her.

One word more about Paris would be superfluous. Such succinctness is why I enjoy reading travel guides and history books. People who don't know how to summarize have no dignity. Neither do people who needlessly drag on their messy lives. They who don't know the beauty of simplification, of pruning away the unnecessary, die without ever comprehending the true meaning of life.

I always take a trip when I'm paid at the completion of a job. This time, I will go to Paris. These few lines in the travel guide are enough to pique my curiosity. I will spend the days reading Henry Miller or Oscar Wilde or sketching Ingres at the Louvre. The man who reads travel guides on a trip is a bore. I read novels when I'm traveling, but I don't read them in Seoul. Novels are food for the leftover hours of life, the in-between times, the moments of waiting.

At the library, I flip through magazines first. Of all the articles, the interviews interest me the most. If I'm lucky, I find clients in them. Reporters, armed with middlebrow, cheap sensibilities, hide my potential clients' characteristics between the lines. They never ask questions like, "Have you ever felt the urge to kill someone?" And obviously they never wonder, "How do you feel when you see blood?" They don't show the interviewees David's or Delacroix's paintings and ask them their thoughts. Instead, the interviews are filled with meaningless chatter. But they can't fool me; I catch the glimmer of possibility in their empty words. I unearth clues from the types of music they prefer, the family histories they sometimes reveal, the books that hit a nerve, the artists they love. People unconsciously want to reveal their inner urges. They are waiting for someone like me.

For example, a client once told me that she liked van Gogh. I asked her whether she liked his landscapes or his self-portraits. She hesitated, then told me she preferred his self-portraits. I always take a close look at those who lose themselves in self-portraits. They are solitary souls, prone to introspection, who have really grappled with their existence. And they know such introspection, though painful, is secretly exhilarating. And if someone asks me the kind of question I myself might pose, I can tell he's lonely. But not all lonely people are suitable clients.

After browsing through magazines, I look through newspapers. I read everything carefully, from obituaries to want ads—especially ads seeking a particular kind of person. I read the business section as well. I focus on articles about once-prosperous companies on the brink of bankruptcy. I also pay close attention to the fluctuations of the stock market, because stocks are the first indicators of social change. In the culture section, I note current trends in the art scene and popular kinds of music. Of course, new books are also a subject of interest. Reading these articles helps me figure out my potential clients' current tastes. My knowledge of their favorite music, art, and books will help the conversation flow freely.

Sometimes, leaving the library, I stop by Insa-dong to look at art or head toward some music megastores to buy CDs. If I'm lucky, I find a potential client roaming the galleries. I look for people absorbed in the thoroughly deliberate study of a piece of art, people who never once glance at their watches—even on a Saturday afternoon. These people have nowhere else to go; they have no one to meet. And the paintings that enthrall them, that hold them rooted completely in one place for a long time, inadvertently betray their viewers' innermost desires.

In the evening I head to my office on the seventh floor of a run-down building downtown. I only have a phone, desk, and computer in my office. I never meet anyone here. I don't even have to see my landlord because I pay my rent online. When I get there, I turn the answering machine off and wait for the phone to ring. By 1:00 A.M., I usually receive around twenty calls. They call responding to my ad in the paper: "We listen to your problems." Having read this simple sentence, they wait until nightfall to dial. I talk until early in the morning to people with various problems: a girl being raped by her father, a gay man about to be conscripted into the army, a woman cheating on her boyfriend, a wife beaten by her husband. I hear stories I'd never discover in the library, bookstore, or Insa-dong galleries during the day. This is how I find the majority of my clients.

After a few minutes, I can figure out anyone's level of education, likes and dislikes, and economic circumstances. I can detect and select a budding client with this kind of information. I like having the power to choose my clients.

But there are pitfalls. The very fact that callers still have the will to converse with someone means they haven't despaired deeply enough to enlist my services. So I take a different tack from that of ordinary counselors, who listen to their stories but don't offer solutions. I listen to them only until I can figure them out, then ply them with my advice. There's no point in continuing to listen to the girl whose father rapes and beats her every night. All I can tell the girl, who is already seventeen, is that she should run away. But ordinary counselors tell her to stay, to suck it up, and to call social organizations or the police for help. These counselors are ignoring the essence of the problem and the simplicity of the solution. It's not as if this girl doesn't know what she should do.

If the caller reacts positively to my provocation, I allow the call to continue. She feels relieved and cleansed. When I think it's the appropriate moment, I slip in: "If he's that kind of father, why not kill him?" If she responds warily, I tell her it was a joke. On the other hand, if she doesn't hang up, it's a sign that she is interested in my methods. But I don't encourage murder. This type of inflammatory comment is merely to weed out the kind of people I don't want. I have no interest in one person killing another. I only want to draw out morbid desires, imprisoned deep in the unconscious. This lust, once freed, starts growing. The caller's imagination runs free, and she soon discovers her potential.

When I think someone has promise, I meet him. Not in my office, of course. Sometimes we go for a drink, or to an exhibition, or to a movie. Sometimes, although rarely, if it's a very important client, we go on a trip together. By important, I don't mean someone who pays a lot of money but someone who stimulates my creativity. It's hard to find someone like this, but when I do, my happiness is bound-less. But I don't reveal this in front of them. They don't know anything about me: not my name, my hometown, the schools I attended, or even my hobbies. I hide my tastes with constant talk. Uncomprehending, they shake their heads at me, because I keep dodging their expectations of who I am. But this is to be expected, as nobody really knows much about a god.

I talk, until the moment I part ways with the client, solely to elicit his family history and childhood years, his love sto-ries, his successes and failures, books he's read, and artists and music he likes. Most people tell you their stories with-out much resistance. When they do, they're honest. Some want to back out of the deal after I listen to all they have to say. I give back their money except for the deposit. But many of those clients come back later. When they do, they follow through with the contract without further discussion.

When I finish a job, I travel. When I come back I write about the client and our time together. Through this act of creation, I strive to become more like a god. There are only two ways to be a god: through creation or murder.

Not all executed contracts become stories. Only clients who are worth the effort are reborn through my words. This part of my work is painful. But this arduous process bears witness to my sympathy and love for my clients.

Shakespeare once said, "Then is it sin / To rush into the secret house of death / Ere death dare come to us?" Hun-dreds of years after the great playwright, the poet Sylvia

Plath took it further. "The blood jet is poetry. / There is no stopping it." The woman who wrote this ended her life by opening the gas valve of her oven.

My clients don't have Sylvia Plath's literary talent, but they design the end of their lives with as much beauty as she did. Their written stories now number more than ten. I plan to slowly release them into the world. I don't need an advance or royalties. I have enough money to support myself. And that wouldn't be respectful of my clients. I plan to put the writings into an envelope, without any conditions or demands, and send them to a publisher. Then I will hide, formless, and watch my creations resurrect.

I turn on the computer and start opening password-protected files. The first file tells the story of a young woman who hired me two winters ago.

PART II

JUDITH

The pain of bewitchment often
Makes me dream of a bird's light body
My jealousy is lighter than air
I want to disappear because I love.

—Yu Ha, "Looking at a Warbler's Nest"

"IT'S SNOWING SO MUCH!"

"..."

"How's K?"

It's already been five hours. Judith and C sit in the idling car on the national highway at the entrance of Hangye Peak. They sit still, doing nothing, periodically turning on the wipers to push away the snow heaped on the windshield. The radio reports that this is the heaviest snowfall in twenty years. Apparently it's caused by the meeting of a front formed in China and an air mass originating in Siberia. The cars on the road don't budge. In snow that comes up to car bumpers, chains are useless.

There aren't any houses nearby. Night is falling. The sky, which was overcast during the day, turns black at 5:00 P.M. C moves to turn on the wipers, but Judith stops him, breaking her long silence.

"Leave it alone. It's better not to see outside."

She files her nails, whistling. Without the wipers, the snow blankets the windshield in a matter of seconds. The inside of the car is almost pitch-black, the headlights only faintly discernible. C can't even see Judith, who's sitting right next to him. He can merely sense the outline of her body. He actually feels comforted. His eyes begin to smart from the dry air inside the car.

"It's like the North Pole here," Judith says, leaning her face on the window.

"The North Pole?"

"You know that guy, Heo Yeong-ho? I watched him get to the North Pole on TV yesterday."

"So?"

"Heo Young-ho was heading to the North Pole, pulling his sled, but apparently the Arctic is a big floating chunk of ice that keeps moving all the time, around and around. So for a while Heo Young-ho just kept circling the North Pole. When he finally got there, he had just enough time to stick a flag into the ground and take a picture before he split. The pole was drifting off to somewhere else right at the next moment."

"The North Pole doesn't move. The ice does."

"Same difference. It's the same thing, whether the ice is moving or we're moving or the North Pole is moving. Don't you ever walk down a street and stop suddenly, looking around, and wonder where you are?"

C vividly remembers the first time he met Judith. It was the day of his mother's funeral. When C came home after the burial, K was having sex with Judith in the living room. They were entangled together, not stopping even when the front door opened and a gust of cold wind reached their naked bodies. A picture of his mother, draped in black ribbon, was looking down at them. K saw him first. He got up with a bored expression on his face and started putting his clothes on, picking them out of the mess of clothing flung around him. Even then, she lay there, her eyes closed. Go into the room, K told her. She finally opened her eyes and looked at C. Her pupils, still brimming with lingering lust, looked blue. She resembled Gustav Klimt's *Judith*, the ancient Israeli heroine who seduced the Assyrian general Holofernes and cut his head off while he was asleep. But Klimt excised Judith's nationalism and heroism and left only fin de siècle sensuality.

The woman resembling Judith scooped up her undergarments and disappeared into the guest room. "Why aren't you coming in?" K asked, as if C, who was still standing at the front door, were the one behaving strangely.

"What are you doing? This is my apartment," C rebuked K in a low voice, and headed uncertainly toward the living room as if he were entering the apartment for the first time.

"I know it is. How did the funeral go? I'm sure it went fine. Funerals and weddings usually end up being fine one way or another."

"Why didn't you come?"

"Will you believe me if I said I didn't feel like it?"

"Yeah. Who is she?"

"Just a girl. She's okay. We're going to stay a few days."

K came home only after receiving news of his mother's death. It had been five years since he had run away from home, dropping out of high school, and he had changed more than C expected. K hung out in C's apartment instead of attending their mother's funeral. Nobody, not even C, tried to dissuade him. And while clumps of dirt fell on their mother's coffin, K was fooling around with Judith in C's apartment. C thought about the hard work he had put into the funeral compared to K's carnal pleasure. He felt tired. He went into his bedroom and fell asleep in his clothes.

The blizzard hasn't slowed. The fuel gauge is now pointing at half a tank. When C turns off the engine to save gas, the inside of the car quickly turns chilly. It was −12°C during the day, so it's probably colder now. He turns on the engine again.

"Are you bored?" he asks Judith, but she doesn't answer. Instead he hears a rustle. A click. She's leaned her seat backward.

"Are you going to sleep?"

"Shh."

Snow piles thickly on the windshield. C feels both nervous and reassured; they're completely cut off from the world. Judith's clothes rustle, faster and faster. She breathes louder. This is what she often does when she's bored.

"Do you want me to turn on some music?"

"Yeah."

He hears affirmation between gasps. He fumbles for a tape and pushes one into the tape deck. It's a B. B. King album. A slow, sticky blues beat fills the sealed car. She mumbles something over and over, like a possessed shaman. "Yeah, yeah, ah, ahh, yes, more, a little more." The car starts to shake. The snow on the windshield slides off, bit by bit. She forcefully takes his right hand and places it on her breast. C slips his hand inside her blouse and starts to fondle her breast, mechanically. He feels a faint wetness. "I'm going to kill you! Kill you!" Her muttering becomes higher pitched. "Aah!" With a short, sharp scream, her undulating body gradually quiets down. C gives her breast a last strong squeeze and removes his hand.

"And still everything's the same, even though I did my best to get as far away as I could. The snow's not stopping either," Judith spits out, smoothing her clothes.

"Where did you go?"

"Somewhere far, far away."

He turns on the radio. The urgent weather report continues. "The snowfall in the Yeongseo area has reached seventy-two centimeters at seven P.M. All train and bus service has stopped in Cheorwon, Inje, and Wontong. Gangwon Province has issued an emergency overtime order to all civil servants and is focusing on clearing the roads, but the work has been delayed due to the continuing blizzard."

"Sir, where to?" K asks his three passengers.

"Pajang-dong, please."

"And you?"

"North Gate."

"Excuse me, where do you want to go?"

"Please let me off at South Gate."

The taxi smells of liquor. The heater roars at full blast to battle the –10°C temperature outside. The dry, impure heat mixed with the customers' wet, alcoholic breath keeps the humidity inside the taxi at an adequate level. K inhales deeply and pulls his seat belt across his shoulder and waist. Constraining his body, strapping it to the body of the car, makes him feel more in tune with the 1994 Stella TX. He steps lightly on the accelerator while still in neutral, and the wheels turn in their place. He feels a gentle vibration. The needle goes up to 4,000 RPM and falls down again with ease. K checks his left mirror, then shifts into first gear and turns the wheel completely. With that, the car lurches forward. His customers, thrown backward, briefly wake up and look around.

It's 1:00 A.M. People who missed the last train for Gyeonggi Province wander around Sadang Station. K shifts into third gear and steps on the gas. He feels a slight uneven vibration from the RPM falling quickly but doesn't give it much thought. His Stella, used to quick accelerations, shoots toward Gwacheon. His taxi is already going 130 kilometers per hour while still in the city. Near the Gwacheon racetrack the light turns red, and the brake lights of the slowing car in front gleam. K quickly looks in his right mirror, changes lanes, and runs the light. The customer sitting beside him glances backward nervously.

K is satisfied with his Stella TX taxi. He knows many who prefer Sonatas or Princes. But there aren't many cars as good as this Stella TX. The structure of its engine is simple. It doesn't break down and the acceleration isn't bad. At the Gwacheon-Uiwang Highway tollbooth, he gives the collector a one-thousand-won bill and gets one hundred won in change. At this point, his muscles start to tense slightly. This section of the highway doesn't get much traffic but has two lanes each way—ideal for bullet taxis. As he steps down on the accelerator, he rolls up his window. The needle goes up to 5,000 RPM. He glances at the customers in the backseat. They're all sleeping, their heads thrown back by the force of the car's motion. Only the customer next to him is awake. He's either not very drunk or is nervous about how fast they're going.

A strong force pulls K's body back as the car accelerates. It's inertia, the tendency to continue movement. His body wants to stay put while the Stella wants to shove him forward. He feels a little dizzy, but it isn't entirely unpleasant. The world has always moved him around quickly, and right now this Stella is his world. Soon he will adapt. The speed of his body will adjust to that of the taxi. The taxi will comply with the law of inertia.

Most of the road between Gwacheon and Uiwang is suspended in the air. Overpasses and trusses support this highway. And the view-blocking, antinoise barrier renders the world below invisible. No one on the ground can see the cars moving, just as the drivers can't see anything below. Low-wattage streetlights are placed only intermittently, so the road is very dark. The headlights shooting out from the front of each car only illuminate the ten meters immediately in front of them. At these speeds, that distance disappears in less than one second—each car racing through the darkness as fast as possible, dashing forward like racehorses with blinders on both sides of their eyes.

"Nine-*pping*."

"Eight."

"I have a pair of deuces. What about you, Kim?"

"Do over."

"Dammit. I wasted the *ttaeng* price."

They are inside a run-down bar, located in the alley next to the twenty-four-hour convenience store in front of Sadang Station. K cautiously picks up two cards. Cherry blossom and clover bush. It's seven *kkeut*. He quickly surveys the others' expressions. Only one has folded, and the others are throwing in thousand-won bills.

"I'm out." K folds. His hand is too weak. The others' eyes shift quickly. Seong-bo Transit driver Lee's eye muscle twitches. He must have a good hand. Lee tosses in a ten-thousand-won bill. Gyeonggi Transit's Kim follows suit. Everyone else is out. Lee reveals his hand. *Gabo*. He wins. Kim only has five *kkeut*. He must have thought that Lee was bluffing. Kim stands up. "Shit, me and my bad luck today! I'm going to go for another round, but be here when I get back."

By the time he returns, they won't be there anymore. Kim knows this, too, so his words are mere filler. When their turn comes, each will get up without any regret to drive his taxi. K gingerly picks up the new hand in front of him. He enjoys this fickle, short-lived tension of a hand of cards. He has one clover bush. He breathes in surreptitiously without letting the others notice, and slowly slides up the other card with his thumb. Another clover bush. He has a pair of fours. He tries not to look at anyone, to ensure that his expression can't be read.

Just one hand is dealt, deciding the course of the set. After that, only deception remains. You can't show your glee when you have a good hand. You also can't look dejected when you have a bad one. But, even more importantly, if you pretend to be let down each time you have a good hand, nobody will believe you after you keep winning despite your reaction. To wear no expression—this is the key.

Is this like life? K wonders. My hand is already determined from the beginning. My hand in life is probably something worthless, like three *kkeut*. There's no chance in hell that a three *kkeut* can beat a pair of aces. There are only two possibilities: either that I'm so lucky with my bluffing that the others with decent hands fold, apprehensively, or the others have worse hands of one or two *kkeut*. But I can only get pennies for that. I can only hope that the round is over quickly and I'm dealt a new hand. But, in the end, even three *kkeut* is fine. I will live in the moment—to the end.

K puts down his pair of fours and waits for the others to bet. The stakes rise to ten thousand won. From his pocket, he takes the twenty thousand won he earned by going down to Suwon earlier that night and drops it on top of the pile. The others glance at him.

"Dammit, I'm betting everything I earned tonight. Fuck it. I'll just have to do another shift," K says, pretending it doesn't matter either way. The others hesitate. This is the climax of the game of *seotta*. When the stakes get higher and the gamblers hesitate, everyday fatigue and boredom evaporate. K's only thinking about the two clover bushes. At this moment, no birds sing and the creek has stopped, as the saying goes. And in the midst of all this, K doesn't even feel himself go hard.

Two players, dubious, toss bills in the middle of the circle, imitating K. K throws down the cards to show his hand.

"Shit, it's a pair of fours." The men's eyes scan K's face rapidly. Having lost not only the bets but also the flush bonus of twenty thousand won each, they wait impatiently for the next hand. These men don't play Go-Stop. Go-Stop, with its unintentional reversals and intense head games, fails to suck them in. And most important, Go-Stop is too damn slow.

The Stella races along the dark road, through the Gwacheon tunnel. People say these taxis "fly." But it may not be a mere simile. It's as if its wheels hover slightly above the road. Every time the wind blows, the car sways a little. Speeding down the highway in the middle of the night, when there aren't any other cars on the road, K often forgets where he's going. His field of vision becomes narrower the faster he drives. The trees and streetlights lining the road lose their shape as the car accelerates. Clinging together like sticky mucus, they melt down behind the car.

Where am I? K shakes his head to snap out of his daze.

The speedometer shows 180 kilometers per hour. The noise of the engine and the wind have swallowed all other sounds. K's ears pop. The hum of speed and his narrower field of vision erase reality. The customer next to him grumbles, but K doesn't pay attention. Suddenly, he sees a truck painfully climbing the incline ahead. He quickly changes lanes and passes the truck. He's alert, his nerves as sharp as a knife blade. His penis hardens; his head is empty. His muscles breathe with the Stella TX, instinctively.

He goes into a phone booth after dropping off his last customer in front of Suwon's South Gate. Nobody picks up. Where's Se-yeon? He tries to light a cigarette, but his lighter doesn't work. The fluid must be out. He tries a few more times, then flings the cigarette and lighter away. He inserts the phone card into the slot again and presses each button deliberately. The few seconds of waiting make him anxious. He tries another number. His brother doesn't answer the phone either. K exits the phone booth, asks a taxi driver for a light, and sticks a lit cigarette between his lips. Did she go to see his brother?

K gets back in the car and races toward Sadang subway station. The radio is reporting a snowstorm in Yeongseo. K detects a tinge of excitement in the voice of the announcer, who is saying that all traffic has stopped. It starts to flurry. Will it snow as much in Seoul? If so, he has to get back before there's too much snow on the ground. K changes into the leftmost lane and speeds up.

When Judith called, C was eating the pizza he had ordered for lunch.

"It's been a long time," she said.

"Has it?" he asked casually, as if he hadn't been thinking about her at all.

"I want to go somewhere. Can you drive me?"

"Where?"

"Jumunjin."

"Why?"

"It's my hometown. And it's my birthday today."

"Come over, then."

"Okay. I'll be there soon."

That's how they decided to go on this trip. The snow started when they passed Yangpyeong. By Hongcheon, it was coming down hard, so they drove on with snow chains strapped onto the tires, but after a while, when they got to where they were now, they couldn't go any farther.

"When did you leave Jumunjin?" C asks.

"Jumunjin?"

"Didn't you say it was your hometown?"

"I just said that because I wanted to go somewhere," Judith replies nonchalantly, and keeps whistling. C can't believe his ears. He takes his hand off the wheel and leans back into the seat. The purpose of the trip has disappeared.

"So it's not your birthday, either?"

"No."

"I see. It's funny, the truth makes people uncomfortable, but a lie gets people excited. Isn't that right?"

"You would have come with me even if I didn't lie."

Perhaps she's right. Sometimes C wishes there were a reason for everything. Like when you find yourself wishing a friend you're drinking with would just suddenly keel over. It's sort of funny to imagine that he'd die from a heart attack and people would come to his funeral, drink together, follow him to his grave site, shovel dirt on his coffin, and ride back in the hearse. But no matter how you die, the world always stays the same. Like this place they're stuck in. Snow keeps falling, almost to the point of annoyance. It's like staring at the same unchanging screen for several hours. Like when the TV shows multicolored stripes before regular programs, the so-called screen adjustment period. C's tired of this darkness. He turns on the wipers and they struggle to push the snow off the windshield. He turns on the dome light. It becomes a little brighter in the car. Judith is lying back in her seat, her skirt hiked up and her blouse open. When C looks at her, she says mechanically, like an answering machine message, "What? You want to do it?"

"I'm tired."

"Let me know if you want to." She closes her eyes again and he turns off the light. He's thirsty. C takes out a lollipop from the glove compartment. When he puts it in his mouth, his saliva pools and his thirst disappears. Judith likes Chupa Chups lollipops. When she isn't smoking she constantly sucks on them. She doesn't take the thing out of her mouth, even during sex. Every time, C is scared that the stick will poke his eye out. Actually, one did stab his left eye once. He worried he might go blind, and he was afraid to have sex with her for a few days.

C woke up late the day after K brought her to his apartment. His head felt leaden and he had no appetite because he had stayed up all night for a few days straight. He was listless but at the same time alert, the consequence of extreme exhaustion. He was in an emotional void, only able to respond to some stimulation. When he stepped into the living room he remembered his brother having sex with a woman the night before, but he was still groggy so it was hard to tell whether he had seen it in real life or in a video.

C made coffee. As the smell of coffee wafted toward the living room, the door of the guest room opened and Judith appeared.

"Can I have a cup, too?"

C poured the rest of the coffee into a cup and handed it to her. Her hair was disheveled and traces of makeup were left on her face, as if she had just woken up. She was wearing denim cutoffs and a baggy T-shirt printed with the name of a prestigious American university on the West Coast. She looked very young in this getup.

"You look like a different person with clothes on," C commented.

"I bet we surprised you yesterday," she said, letting out a laugh, weak and leaky like a broken humidifier. "I've heard a lot about you."

"Where's K?" C asked, glancing toward the guest room.

"He went to work."

"What work?"

"Didn't you know? He's a bullet."

"A bullet?"

"You know, a bullet taxi driver. Bang!" Judith made a gun with two fingers and mimed shooting C. C jumped despite himself, and at that moment the image of her naked body lying in the living room flashed in his head. He sensed that he was about to make a dangerous choice. He was attracted to his brother's girl, this woman who resembled Judith. But he didn't want to blame it on the fatigue sweeping over him after the funeral.

Judith finished her coffee, took out a Chupa Chups from her pocket, and stuck it in her mouth. For the first few minutes, she seemed to concentrate her whole being on eating the candy. She stared intently at the stick, almost cross-eyed. C hadn't met a woman who ate candy in a while. He despised women who chewed gum. You don't need imagination to chew gum. You endlessly work your mouth but always come back to the same place. He realized that the image he wanted to see was that of a woman eating candy, savoring it slowly—just as she did. His attention strayed to her from the morning paper he had been reading. She continued to lick, then stretched and lengthened her body. She put her feet on the coffee table and leaned back as far as possible into the sofa, and kept sucking.

"That was a game," Judith says, breaking the silence. The windshield is again covered in thick snowdrifts, and the inside of the car returned to its pitch-black state. "When I slept with you for the first time, I mean. Remember I was eating a lollipop? I knew you were looking at me. So I decided to play a game and see whether I would win you over while I was eating candy, or afterward. I decided that if you came over to me while I was eating it, I would live with you, and if you came to me after I was done, I would live with K. Fun, huh?"

She rolls down the window. A cold gust and snow rush in. She reaches up to the top of the car, grabs a fistful of snow, and rolls up the window. She turns on the light.

"I just thought of something fun to do," she says, packing the snow into a small ball, the size of a golf ball. She parts her legs, giggling. The snowball slides up inside of her. She still has a lollipop in her mouth. She shivers. Her brow is furrowed for a long time, as if she can still feel the snow on her skin.

————

That day, when C saw Judith's left hand undoing the button of her shorts and sliding inside, he stood up. She didn't stop, her right hand curled around the lollipop stick, her left touching herself. C didn't know where to go. He stood there for a while, watching her movements become faster and her expression change. It seemed that a very long time had passed. She opened her eyes. Their eyes met. She called him over. He went to her, and she pointed to her back. He held her from behind. Even then, she was writhing violently. He worried that she might be going insane. After a while, she relaxed in his arms. He laid her on the sofa and inserted his dick inside of her. She sucked her lollipop, bored, even as he thrusted. He came before she finished her candy. He immediately stood up and went to take a shower. He faintly remembers hearing her laughter behind him and, for some reason, wanting to listen to Mozart.

The fuel gauge shows that there's only a quarter of a tank left. They will freeze to death when the gas runs out. C turns down the heat. The snow isn't stopping. It's coming down heavily, like the fake snow used in movies. Judith is touching up her makeup, using the mirror on the sunshade.

"Why do you bother fixing your makeup?" C asks.

"I have nothing else to do."

"We're running out of gas."

"Are we going to die here?" she asks, penciling in her eyebrows. She looks serious, probably unsatisfied with the eyebrows she's drawing.

"It's possible."

"Cool. We'll be smothered to death by snow."

"Maybe we should walk and try to find a village. There must be something if we walk along the road."

"I don't want to." Done with her eyebrows, she's touching up her lips.

"Why not?"

"It's cold out."

"When we run out of gas it's going to be cold in here, too. And aren't you hungry?"

"A little, but I can wait. Turn on the radio."

Finished with her makeup, she smells like an apple. After his mother's body was embalmed it also smelled of apple. Apples emit an intense scent as they rot. On the radio, a dance music group is laughing with a female DJ. She's talking about the weather. "I hear that a snowstorm has hit Yeongdong and Yeongseo. Are you going to go skiing?"

"It's hard to find time because we're so busy. We all really like to ski but we haven't been in a while."

"Oh, that's too bad!" The DJ sounds hyper. "Okay, let's hear a song, then we'll continue our conversation." A song by the group that had just been joking around comes out of the radio. Compared to the upbeat rhythm, the lyrics are dull, going on about first love.

"Do you remember your first guy?" C leans his face on the steering wheel.

"No. It was one guy out of two, but I don't exactly remember which one it was. I was sixteen and the three of us lived together for about a month. I ended up sleeping with both but I can't really remember who was first. I'm always like that. I never remember anything once it's over. I mix up movie plotlines, and a lot of times I watch a video I've seen before because I don't remember the title. I guess there hasn't been anything worth remembering. But sometimes weird things stay in my memory for a long time. TV shows like *Heo Yeong-ho's North Pole Expedition* or *Animal Kingdom*. I don't like dramas or novels. The only thing I watch religiously is *Animal Kingdom*. Did you know the lioness is in charge of hunting, but the male lion always eats first? After the males are full, the females and the cubs eat. My mom was the breadwinner in my family, too. Maybe because of that my dad always crept around like a loser. Once he was caught sleeping with a bar girl and my mom clobbered his face with an ashtray. But now I can't really remember either of their faces."

"Why did you leave home?"

"At school my teacher asked me why I didn't have my book with me. I told him my dad ripped it up, and he asked me why. So I said he rips up books whenever he drinks, and he told me I was lying. I yelled that I wasn't, and he hit me, saying that I was being rude. I didn't go back to school after that. The teacher called when I missed classes several days in a row, and then my mom beat the hell out of me. So I ran away. It was great. Nobody bothered me and I could drink and buy clothes and sleep with boys."

"Don't you miss your mom?"

"You're just like everyone else, asking that kind of question. You don't understand. Don't ask things like that. I hate people who ask questions. Guys who ask questions have a lot to hide. Instead of saying something about themselves, they always want someone else to talk, to reveal something about themselves."

The radio weather forecast says that over thirty centimeters of snow are predicted to fall before it stops.

The snowfall has become heavy by the time he gets to Sadang Station. K parks and ducks into a makeshift bar, set up on the side of the street. "One bottle of *soju* and some boiled squid, please," K orders.

The squid is lying quietly on the plate. It's tame, its body cut in horizontal strips. K remembers the time he went to Jumunjin with Se-yeon. Before sunrise the squid boats came into the brightly lit docks. The squid, thrown in heaps on the docks, moved about, tangled together. A few squirted black ink. He and Se-yeon drank *soju,* eating raw strips of squid. She seemed to be at home at the harbor. He asked her if she was from Jumunjin, but she didn't answer. She smelled like C's lotion. He asked her if she'd slept with his brother. She nodded. The scent of C's lotion cut through the fishy smell of the ocean, and K started to feel sick to his stomach.

There aren't any customers in the bar. Perhaps it's because of the snow. K throws back two shots, then eats some of the squid. The bar where he first met Se-yeon is somewhere around here. He and the other drivers had gone there for karaoke. The five men entered a room and ordered beer, and Se-yeon came in to peel fruit for them. She peeled apples awkwardly. She looked young, despite her dark purple eye shadow. She didn't laugh once. The drivers got pissed and cursed at her, a woman selling a good time who didn't laugh. The owner of the karaoke bar came in and cursed at her, too. He dragged her outside, and they could hear him slapping her. A bit later, when she came back in, she laughed endlessly. She laughed at a lame joke, when someone groused about the taxi dispatcher, and when someone said that the Korean soccer team was likely to get to the World Cup. The drivers got pissed again. Someone called her a crazy bitch. She laughed at that, too, and was dragged out again.

After all the drivers went home, K went back to that place, paid, and took her out. It's my birthday today, Se-yeon said. So they drank some more and slept together in a motel near Sadang Station.

"Why didn't you laugh at first?" K wondered.

"Because nothing was funny."

"Then why did you laugh afterward?"

"Because it was all funny then."

She said it was her birthday whenever he went to see her, so each time they drank and slept together.

That very morning, she'd said it was her birthday again. So K had sex with her before going to work. He gets aroused when she says it's her birthday.

"I don't have any more Chupa Chups. This is the last one," she said during sex.

"I'll get you some when I get off work," K told her.

In the bar, K fumbles with the bag of Chupa Chups next to him. He takes one out, peels off the wrapper, and puts it in his mouth.

But where is she now? Is she with C? C always takes everything. K is used to this. Some people take things as if that's the most natural act in the world. When he thinks about his older brother, all of his memories are about having things stolen from him. When he was very young, before he started going to school, they had a puppy. The puppy was cute, with fluffy brown fur. It was always in C's arms. K tried hard to win its affections, but the puppy would always run back to his brother. Even to this day, K doesn't know why; he doesn't want to know.

That puppy disappeared one summer day. After the rainy season it was found in the mouth of the drainpipe coming down from the mountain. The adults said that it must have crawled into the narrow sewer and was unable to come back out again. Fluffy had rotted, his guts burst, in the corner of a drain for an entire summer. Nobody removed his body. K couldn't understand C, who was able to finish his bowl of rice the night they found Fluffy. K couldn't eat for two days.

Their father was in the military, so they always lived in the military compound. Whether he hated or loved him, C was K's only friend. But he had to pay a price to play with C.

C would always want to bet when they played Chinese chess or children's Go. C always won. Even if K really won, somehow C ended up winning anyway. Those who always come out ahead in the end are a different breed. The foreign stamps that a cousin gave K soon became C's. K remembers the German stamps with cars on them. He wants to see them again. And butterflies. C's butterflies, pinned and rendered into ash.

Once, hearing these stories, Se-yeon remarked, "You guys must have fought a lot."

"No, by the time I entered middle school I never fought with C."

"Why not?"

"When our father beat me for my bad grades, smoking, or because I ran away, C always stopped him. He would calm our father down and come to talk to me gently. Each time C convinced me to shape up. I always thought he was the only one who understood me, and when I left home I missed C the most. Still, when I think about him I get the feeling there's something a little off. You have to be careful with him . . ."

Se-yeon giggled. "Stupid, those guys are the scariest. They're the most frightening customers I have at the bar. These assholes look after me when I'm in trouble. They hold me when I'm tired and wipe my tears when I cry. But they're the ones who get mad when I eat a lollipop during sex. They try to get away with not paying for motels, and in the morning they tell me they don't have cab fare. Most often, the guys who bought me a meal when I was really broke were the violent ones, dragging me by the hair and all that."

But it's true that K missed his brother when he left home five years ago. Around the time he stopped missing C, he started fixing cars. He lived in a room in the corner of a garage, a huge poster of a Lamborghini hanging from his wall. During the day his entire body was coated in grease as he changed the oil in people's cars, but he spent his evenings dreaming. He read and reread the automotive magazines distributed free at garages. He memorized the specs of the Mercedes 500. He was contemptuous of the cars he fixed for customers. He found his customers laughable for bringing in cars that could only hit 180 kilometers per hour and fussing about small problems.

Once he saw a Porsche. The man who got out of the car sauntered into the shop, bought antifreeze, and left. He was in his early thirties. How could he drive a Porsche and have such a nonchalant expression on his face? K couldn't understand it. When the man turned on the engine after putting the antifreeze in the trunk, that powerful purr was different from any other engine he'd heard. He realized that he wanted to kill someone for the first time in his life. He was so shocked by this impulse that he tore up his poster of the Lamborghini into bits that night, sobbing.

K is drinking his second bottle of *soju*. The squid is still mostly untouched. There are only two older men drinking in the bar. They are talking about Dok Islet. The balding man is saying that Japan should be bombed. The other man agrees, and adds that Korea should hurry up and develop nuclear weapons. The snow starts falling harder. K takes another Chupa Chups and puts it in his mouth. He sees double—two owners of the bar. Either his right or left eye has shifted to the outer corner of its socket. He momentarily sees the world askew.

"Isn't it uncomfortable to see double?" Se-yeon asked curiously one time, studying his wayward eye.

"When I'm comfortable, the muscle in my eye relaxes and one eye rolls to the side. It's been like this since I was a kid. When I concentrate on it, it comes back to normal. Or else everything looks overlapped. But it doesn't bother me. I just choose one of the images and go with that."

Se-yeon shook her head as if she couldn't believe it.

"Nobody knows, other than my family. When I'm with other people I make sure to tense my eyes," K explained.

"Doesn't it make you tired?"

"Life is tiring. I'm used to it, anyway."

"If you don't show it to anyone, why do you show it to me?"

"Because of your Chupa Chups."

K closes his eyes and downs the rest of the soju. He pays and goes into a phone booth. He dials slowly. Nobody answers. Not Se-yeon, not C—nobody answers his calls. The world doubles again. K yanks the Chupa Chups from his mouth and flings it outside the phone booth. He weaves over to his car and sits in the driver's seat. Snow is gathering on his windshield. He turns on the engine and the radio. The weather reporter is saying that mountain villages are stranded because of the snowstorm in Yeongdong and Yeongseo, and the Taebaek and Jungang Railway Lines are out of service. They read names of people missing in a landslide. Some places don't have electricity or telephone service; schools are being closed. K shifts into first gear and steps on the gas. He hears the whirring noise of the wheels turning in vain, then the Stella TX starts to move.

"We're almost out of gas," C says.

"I want to go to the North Pole. They say there's only snow and ice—all white. And polar bears wander around and strong winds blow up to thirty meters per second. In the summer, it's always bright out and the North Pole itself is always floating around on the ocean. Isn't that cool? And sometimes the ice cracks and sinks."

"I'm not kidding. We're stranded," C insists. "It's going to keep snowing and the roads are blocked. We have to go now if we want to live."

"I think all guys are just nervous when they have to stay in one place. I mean, even when they drink they like to go from bar to bar. Why bother leaving? I like it here. It's cozy, like a grave. Have you ever been inside a coffin? When I was in middle school we went on a church field trip and we were all supposed to take turns lying in a coffin. And then we had to talk about what that was like. I think they wanted us to experience death early to make us believe in Jesus more. What do you think I said afterward? I said it was so comfortable. And it really was so cozy that I didn't want to leave. I think a nun asked me if I was scared that I would go to hell. I don't think there is such a thing. But I do want to go to the Arctic. I would like to be bored for eternity. And the North Pole, it doesn't even move."

"There is no North Pole. Didn't you say that the whole thing is a block of ice that floats around on the ocean? If nobody else can find it, you won't get there, either."

The engine shuts off. The lights blink, then fade away. The white LCD of the radio disappears. Only the red anti-theft light blinks periodically. Everything turns pitch-black, like in a blackout drill. It becomes completely quiet. Neither C nor Judith says a word. The cold starts to crawl toward them, like an army of white ants.

"Let's go," C suggests.

"Not yet."

"When?"

"I want to stay a little longer. Hey, do you want to have sex?"

He hears her skirt go down, rustling. Judith pulls his shoulders toward her. He climbs over the emergency brake, squeezing next to her. He settles into the passenger seat and she straddles him, facing out. Holding her from behind, he starts having slow, tedious sex with her. Sometimes her head bumps the ceiling and snow falls off the windshield, but they still can't see anything. A quiz show plays on the radio, which is still working even though the car is turned off. The first caller says the answer is Antonio Banderas. The DJ perkily says it's the wrong answer. He tells the caller that he'll still give him a bookstore gift certificate, and the guy is thrilled. The second caller guesses Leonardo Di-Caprio. The DJ screams that it's the correct answer, clapping. The prize is a CD player. The winner says she'll give it to her sister as a wedding present.

"Why aren't you coming?" Judith asks, at the end of a long, dull thrust. C remembers he's having sex with her.

"I'm not turned on."

"Then try choking me. That'll turn you on."

C starts to pump away again, choking her. He hears her strain for breath a few times, and he becomes nervous, worrying that she might die. He comes quickly. She coughs a few times, then climbs into the backseat.

"You'll never be able to kill anyone," she announces. "There are two kinds of people. Those who can kill and those who can't. The second kind is worse. K's the same way. You guys seem different, but deep down, you're identical. And people who can't kill can't ever truly love."

C falls asleep mulling over her words. He's tired and spent.

He dreams one dream after another, only remembering the last one. On a white snowy field, a neon sign blinks: "North Pole." The sign brightens one second, dims the next, announcing the North Pole like it's Las Vegas. As he walks toward the sign, he sees Judith and a polar bear having sex. C shoots the polar bear. With a bang, the bear falls over and Judith glares at him resentfully. When he goes to flip the bear over, it has changed into K. K is bloody, his eyes wide open and glaring. Naked, Judith stabs C's eyes with a long knife. He sees her knife coming out of the back of his head, all the way through his skull. How can he see the tip of the knife coming out of the back of his head, when his eyes are in front? Even in his dream he tries to figure this out.

The noise of something falling wrenches C from his dream. He's still in the dark car. He's suddenly unbearably cold, probably because his sweat is drying in the cold. He hears the noise again, a branch breaking. He opens the window and looks outside, hearing another thud. Snow, piled on a branch, is falling on the car.

"Aren't you cold?" C asks Judith.

"..."

"Let's go."

"..."

No answer. C feels around the backseat. He doesn't find anything. He forces the car door open, pushing against the piles of snow. He opens the trunk and takes out a flashlight. It looks like the back door has been opened. He sees a winding path through the snow, which comes up to his thighs.

"Se-yeon!" he yells, and starts following the footprints. The path is surprisingly long; he can't see the end. He comes back to the car, shuts the trunk, and gathers his things. He locks the car because he doesn't know how far she's gone.

The wind stings C's eyes. The snowstorm, although it has lightened a bit, continues to blind him. C wades through the snow, the flashlight in one hand, his bag and her purse in the other. It seems to take him a full minute to go forward just ten meters. How did she get through all this snow? He starts to get annoyed. The memory of the last time they had sex and the scenes in his dream float in front of his eyes, jumbled together. But only for a moment. His efforts at fighting through the snow have left him covered in sweat, which drips into his eyes. How far did she go? He starts to tire, and tells himself he doesn't care where she is. She's like mildew that has invaded his life. She's the kind of mold that wouldn't have appeared if he lived austerely, the kind that breeds only in the dark, neglected corners of a building. She has infected his life, not caring what he wants. He hates himself for trudging through the snow looking for a woman who was having sex with his brother on the day their mother was buried. *Seriously, I don't want to know where she is and whether she's dead or alive.* Still, even as he thinks this, he advances, putting one foot in front of the other.

He sees an amber glow far away. The light comes toward him, following the road. It's a snowplow. He signals with his flashlight to stop it.

"Did you see a woman walk by?" C asks the workers.

"A woman with long hair?"

"Yeah, that's her."

The workers point behind them, where they came from. "She was riding a snowplow going to Wontong."

"Where are you guys headed?"

"We're going toward Inner Mount Seorak, so it's the opposite way."

He isn't sure if the woman going the other way is Judith, but he clambers on top of the snowplow. Twenty minutes later, he gets off in front of a restaurant attached to a gas station and stays overnight. When he wakes up the next morning, most of the snow has been cleared from the roads. Gathering his things, he sees her purse lying in a corner of the room. He takes out her identification card from her wallet. She was born on January 21, 1975, in Jumunjin, in Myeongju County, Gangwon Province.

Back in Seoul, C never sees Judith again. He sometimes thinks about her, the woman who, on her birthday, disappeared into the snow, going in the opposite direction of her hometown. He lives his life without ever again seeing the woman who sucked on Chupa Chups during sex. And he sees the North Pole more and more often in his dreams. He always shoots the polar bear against the backdrop of the sun hanging low, and the bear always turns into K's corpse. Only now Judith laughs. And so each day passes. And nothing has changed.

PART III

EVIAN

I sleep very late. I commit suicide at 65%. My life is very cheap, it's only 30% of life for me. My life has 30% of life. It lacks arms, strings, and a few buttons. 5% is devoted to a state of semi-lucid stupor accompanied by anemic crackling. This 5% is called DADA. So life is cheap. Death is a bit more expensive. But life is charming and death is equally charming.

—Tristan Tzara,
"How I Became Charming, Likeable and Delightful"

I'M ALMOST DONE EDITING THE NOVEL. I'll be able to finish it in a week at the latest. I turn off the computer and step out onto the balcony to breathe in the change in season. It's already spring. I have more clients this time of year—because people are afraid of spring, not because they're reacting to the tedium of winter. It's not unusual to be depressed in winter, but with the advent of spring, people are expected to perk up. This expectation makes my clients feel more isolated. Everyone is imprisoned during winter; only those who can't help but be trapped are imprisoned in spring.

I remember once seeing a farmer's squat shanty, roofed with shingles, deep in the mountains. The house was particularly memorable because it contained everything under one roof: animal pens, kitchen, living area, heating system, and a storage room for grains. Because of its confined structure, the smoke coming from the furnace couldn't easily escape the house. The smoke leaked out only after going through the chimney and heating the interior of the house. The snow, the first of which fell in October, kept the family inside. But as soon as it started to melt, all the farmers would rush out of their shingled houses and set fire to the mountain greenery to clear the land, like they were taking part in a festival. The crackling flames would shimmer between the valleys. But nowadays no one can hold such a festival. You can't burn up the land just because the dull winter has passed. Now people resort to setting themselves on fire.

I met Judith in the spring. It was April; the sun was warm, but there was a nip in the wind. That day, I was watching a movie in a theater on Daehak Street. Three characters were in the movie—two men and a woman. One man is the woman's relative as well as the other man's friend. The woman works at a burger joint, and the two men are unemployed. The three rent a car with money they won gambling and go on a trip. The movie was Jim Jarmusch's *Stranger Than Paradise*. Not once do we see the main characters close up. The moviegoers get bored because they can't really see the actors' expressions, and the actors themselves appear to be just as bored. The only escape in their dull lives is gambling or going on trips. Even if they win money by gambling, they then gamble it away again. Even when they go on trips, nothing is ever different. "This is the lake," the woman says in Cleveland, but the lake is indistinguishable: frozen over in a blizzard. You can't see a thing. One of the men grumbles that nothing's changed even though they had come this far. In this movie, there aren't even any of the romance or sex scenes that proliferate in modern cinema. I'm sure the audience wouldn't notice if you swapped the last scene of the movie with the first.

Not surprisingly, only three people were in the movie theater that day. A woman sat three rows in front of me. It was Judith. She dozed off throughout the movie but didn't leave the theater. She didn't even get up after the movie was over. So I watched the movie twice. When the woman said for the second time, "This is the lake," Judith got up from her seat, stumbling a little. A sudden clatter reverberated in the theater; she must have stepped on an empty can. I followed her out. It was just after ten. She walked slowly toward Marronniers Park, bumping into people twice. She went into a phone booth, picked up the receiver, but then put it down.

She walked on for a long time, finally settling down at an outdoor concert in Marronniers Park. Two men with acoustic guitars were singing onstage.

"You come to some place new, and everything looks just the same, right?" I asked, sitting down next to her.

"Yeah," she replied, continuing to gaze at the singers. "Hey," she said, taking out a cigarette.

"Yes?"

"Have you ever wanted to go to the North Pole?" She blew out white smoke.

"You want to go to the North Pole?"

"I went there for a few days once," she said, giggling. "It was really nice. The whole world was covered in white snow. If you stare at the snow for a long time, everything turns dark. Did you know the sunrise is different there? It rises from the sky and falls back into the sky. During winter, it comes up from below your feet and sinks down into the ground. Isn't that amazing?" She looked at me for the first time.

I nodded, agreeing with her. "People say that nobody dies in the North Pole. I know someone who's been there. When she was young she went on a cruise in the Arctic Ocean with her husband, but the ship struck a rock and her husband fell into the ocean and disappeared. In her sixties, she went back on a cruise ship touring the Arctic Ocean, probably to remember her late husband. She was on the deck, looking out to sea, when she saw an ice floe coming from a distance. Her husband was lying on it. When she saw him close up, she jumped into the water."

"Why?"

"He was still in his twenties, frozen in time, and she had gotten old."

She nodded. "That makes sense. I understand how she felt."

Sometimes fiction is more easily understood than true events. Reality is often pathetic. I learned at a very young age that it was easier to make up stories to make a point. I enjoy creating stories. The world is filled with fiction anyway.

We watched the guitarists sing their last song, pack up their guitars and mics, and leave. I stood up and handed her my business card.

"Give me a call if you want to tell someone that you don't want to talk."

She looked down at the card. "What if I don't even feel like saying that I don't want to talk?"

"Is that how you feel now?"

"I don't feel that apathetic. But I think I will soon." She laughed for the first time. It was crumbly like days-old snow.

"Follow me," I ordered, grabbing her hand and pulling her up. She walked beside me without a word. She sank into the passenger seat of my car. When I turned on the engine, we heard Chet Baker's low, gravelly voice.

"Do you know who this is?" I asked.

With difficulty, she slowly shook her head. "I don't know who it is but he makes me feel like the core of the earth is sucking my body in, like I'm going to disappear."

"It's Chet Baker, a jazz musician. He didn't lead a very illustrious life. He was famous for some time, but he won't go down in jazz history. He didn't sing that well and he wasn't the greatest trumpeter. He only played to pay for his drug habit in the sixties."

"Then why do you have his CD?"

"I came across this album cover in a record store. It was a picture of this old, scruffy, unshaven man, his hair slicked back, showing all of his wrinkles. A black-and-white photo reveals a person's shadows. You can understand someone's life from each wrinkle. But his eyes had caught the flash of the camera and were sparkling, and they were so clear. I knew as soon as I saw that picture that this guy was ready to die."

"How could you tell?"

"His eyes were shining with a final hope. Some things can't be hidden even by fatigue-soaked wrinkles. That kind of hope is for rest, not for life."

The second track of the CD came on. It was Baker's famous "My Funny Valentine." The title indicates a light theme, but his voice is low and sorrowful. The song isn't sweet or cheap. It reveals the maturity of a man who has suffered, the generosity of a man who has transcended greed.

"This is a live album of his final concert. Two weeks later he jumped out of his hotel window," I explained.

"Why did he jump?"

"The Amsterdam police concluded it was an accident. But I don't think it was. The more I listen to this album and look at his picture on the cover, the more I think he chose to go."

"Did he leave a will?" she wondered.

"No, but I think this album was like his will, his last words. Some people communicate through writing, but others through their music. I think it's significant that it was recorded at a concert, not in a studio. The texture is different. Don't you think there's more feeling involved if you perform your last song in front of an audience instead of playing it in a sterile studio for some unknown future listener?"

"I guess you're right."

I drove her home. She lived in a rental apartment in the suburbs. I drank coffee in her living room, surrounded by cheap metal furniture and a fourteen-inch TV. She sat by me with a Chupa Chups in her mouth. And when dawn neared, Judith decided to be my client. Three days later, I executed the contract. I boarded a plane to Vienna with her story nestled in my heart.

Vienna is a charming city, with ideas and people trickling through to other places. Ideas like religious reform, Expressionism, and Nazism spread to the rest of the world through this city. Now they call it the gateway between Eastern and Western Europe. Most travelers get visas in Vienna to go to the Czech Republic and Hungary. In Vienna, Hitler aspired to be an artist. "If fate didn't choose me to be the Führer, I would have become Michelangelo," Hitler announced confidently. Mozart also studied in Vienna. Hitler showed a knack for fascism and mob mentality while Mozart earned fame as a composer and performer. Both held an innate talent for captivating the public. But it was easy to move people back in those days, like the way Anne Frank's diary touched a nerve because of the Holocaust. But now it isn't so easy.

Death has become pornographic, shown live on TV. Massacres, which used to be unearthed through rumor, are quickly reported in detail via satellite.

Many different things coexist in Vienna. The traces of the Roman Empire, Nazi relics, and the glory of the House of Hapsburg are all jumbled together. Many people treat this small neutral country's capital as a stopping place, a place to go through on their way to elsewhere. In Vienna, I feel like I could sleep with anyone. I imagine meeting someone, going to a musical like *The Phantom of the Opera*, drinking a glass of beer, having sex on a creaky bed in a pension nearby, and in the morning, each boarding trains headed opposite directions.

I went to Vienna because of my client, Judith. As soon as I carried out my contract, I felt an urge to go to the homeland of Gustav Klimt, who painted the historical Judith. Klimt, who painted in the late nineteenth and early twentieth centuries, was an aesthete, a typical fin de siècle artist. He created exuberant paintings. His *Judith* depicted the peak of decadence, enhanced by its background of decorative, dazzling patterns.

"He called me Judith," Judith told me.

"Why?"

"He said I looked like the Judith drawn by some artist."

That final night with Judith, I understood who that "some artist" was. "It's probably Gustav Klimt."

Inspired by the Bible, countless artists drew Judith, but she resembled Klimt's *Judith*, no one else's.

"It doesn't matter who the artist is. But I'm glad I know his name, now. I'm sure I'll forget it, though." Judith laughed.

To see Klimt's *Judith*, I went to the Museum of Applied Arts in Belvedere Palace. The palace appeared in the distance as the tram looped downtown and entered the southern part of the city. I entered the museum slowly. It was crowded with children on a field trip and tourists sweeping the scene with camcorders. The Japanese cameras that used to proliferate in these places have almost all been replaced by camcorders. Like a magic lamp, the camcorder swallows the palace and sucks in the pond in front. In these tourists' minds, the Belvedere is reduced into an unfocused square image, cast with a bluish tint. The present is re-created to immortalize memories. It's pathetic, but that's human tendency now.

Fortunately, most people were clustered around Klimt's *The Kiss*. *Judith* drew far fewer viewers. Her dark hair is unrealistically big and puffy. Behind her, the gold patterns turn the ornate painting even more extravagant. And her eyes. Her cheeks are flushed, but her eyes are downcast, perhaps open, perhaps closed. She seems to be welcoming the sensation right before orgasm, reveling in that moment. Her lips are slightly parted, relaxed. Her revealed breast is tinted blue. That bluish color, subtly, oppressively radiating, is the energy of death. Judith looks dead, though she is too sensual to be a corpse (or maybe that makes her more attractive). Her left hand holds up the head of Holofernes, whom she has beheaded. The black-haired man is dead, his eyes closed.

Judith killed Holofernes, an enemy leader, after seducing him. But it isn't clear if she still felt traces of desire after his death or if she had reached orgasm at the exact moment of his decapitation.

I was completely captivated by this painting when a woman stepped in front of me. She was Asian, short, and her straight hair was cropped into a bob. She was blocking the bottom of the painting. I moved to the side. Her eyes and face suggested Southeast Asian ancestry. At that point, a guided tour group streamed in to stand in front of *Judith*, so I left the room. I was parched. My client Judith and Klimt's *Judith* danced in front of my eyes and made me dizzy. I went down to the café in the basement and ordered an Evian and a *salade aux lardons*. The Evian, collected in the Alps, tasted a little strong compared to Korean water. But it was lucky that I was able to get an Evian. I often have to settle for carbonated water in Europe.

Once, I went to Prague with a Dutch woman I met traveling. Before disappearing into our respective hotel rooms, we agreed to have tea in the downstairs lounge the next morning. We got to the lounge around eleven. It was a fancy establishment, with a string quartet and a cover. I was shocked when the Dutch woman casually ordered mineral water at a high-class place like that.

Around the time I finished my salad, the Southeast Asian woman entered the café. She bought a Coke and two croissants, and ate slowly. I looked her over carefully. I was sure there had to be something about her that resembled Judith, but I couldn't put my finger on it.

When she finished eating, she flipped through the muscum viewing guide she'd purchased. Her gaze didn't leave Klimt's works. I initiated conversation. Vienna, especially in a Viennese art museum, is a good place to chat up strangers.

"Do you like Klimt?"

The woman looked me in the eye and answered, "No."

"But why are you only looking at his paintings?"

"It's none of your business."

Her accent soared with a Chinese inflection. She might have been from Singapore, or Hong Kong, or Macao. She poured Coke into her glass and drank it. Thanks to my attempt at a conversation, I could now stare sitting across the table from her. Her unmade face was freckled and darkly tanned. It dripped with unhidden fatigue. I wanted to spend the night with her, to welcome dawn with my arm under her travel-weary head. I focus on myself when I travel. My life in Korea is devoted to separating those who could become clients from those who couldn't. I don't live that way when I am abroad.

"Where are you from?"

"Hong Kong," she answered curtly. "What about you?"

"Me? I'm from Hell."

She frowned, then laughed. "So you live in an interesting place."

"It's boring there. Nothing ever changes. So, I guess you're traveling. Where were you before coming to Vienna?"

"Berlin. It rained for three whole days. The only thing I saw was the hotel bar." She closed her visitor's guide, took out a Marlboro, and lit it. "What do you do?"

What do I do? Sometimes I say I'm a therapist, sometimes I say I'm a writer. But I still pause every time I get this question.

"I'm a novelist."

"Have your books been published in English or Chinese?"

"No."

She appeared to lose interest. I get this a lot when I travel. A novelist without a book published in English is treated like a bum.

"What about you?"

"I've done a lot of things. I worked in a department store, for one. There are a lot of department stores in Hong Kong."

"Can I ask how old you are?"

"Twenty-one."

I was a little taken aback. She looked too unhappy to be twenty-one.

"Is this your first time in Vienna?" I asked.

"Yeah. It's not easy to get out of Hong Kong. This is my first time abroad."

Some people live in one city their entire lives. For people in Seoul it would be unimaginable to stay put for two whole decades. I studied this woman from Hong Kong, a part of both Britain and China; a city and a country at the same time. She told me she'd lived in crowded Hong Kong her entire life.

"Where are you staying?" I asked.

She took out a map to check. "A pension on Mariahil-ferstrasse."

Mariahilferstrasse connected the heart of the city to Vienna's western district. A lot of cheaper lodging was clustered there, and her pension wasn't too far from my hotel.

"Do you want to go sightseeing with me tomorrow? This is my third time in Vienna," I offered.

"Sure, why not."

"Let's meet in front of the Vienna Opera House at ten." I marked the location of the Opera House on her map. She opened her small eyes wide and looked at the map, then stood up. I went back to my hotel, packed, and went down to the bar for some beer. A fat old woman tending bar poured me a beer, topped with dense foam, with an experienced air. I took out the *Judith* postcard I'd bought at the museum and gazed at it.

"Is there any special way you want it?" I asked Judith on her last day. Judith stared at me blankly, as if she didn't want to think about it, then pushed the decision on me. This happens quite often, so I wasn't flustered.

"What do you think would be the best for me?" she asked.

"Why don't we start by eliminating the methods you don't like?" I took out my laptop and opened images I presented to clients.

"You don't want to be hanged, do you?" I double-clicked on the first picture file, a picture of a dead person hanging from a tree on a hill.

"No, I don't think I'd like that feeling on my neck." She touched her neck with her left hand.

"It's actually pretty simple. People think you're in pain for a few minutes and die, but that's not right. If you put a noose around your neck and kick away the chair, the noose catches your neck and breaks it. At that point, most people lose consciousness. That's why some people die even though their feet are on the ground. If it took three or four minutes of kicking around to die, that wouldn't be possible."

"I still don't like that option."

I opened the next file. A man was sprawled in a tub filled with pink water.

"This method has usually been used in the West. Roman aristocrats favored it. Your blood circulates faster when you're immersed in hot water and your death comes quicker. It takes a lot to cut your artery, but once you do it, it's very relaxing. You can die watching your blood seep into the water. You'll be in a state of shock because of the amount of blood you lose and you'll feel weaker and weaker, and hazy. But I don't recommend it."

"Why not?"

"A few of my clients insist on slitting their wrists but then ask me to do the cutting. I don't like to have blood on my hands. And participating actively ruins the significance of my work."

"I guess that's true. So you don't do it?"

"I never do anything I shouldn't do."

"So did they end up choosing another method?"

"No. They were able to do it on their own. Though we had to talk more before they could."

"I see."

The way Judith looked right at that moment is seared in my memory. She was vivacious. She was showing me a side of her that made her a completely different person from when I first met her.

"This is exciting. My life has always been an uncontrollable mess. I'm always somewhere I don't want to be. But it feels different now," she said, minutely upbeat.

Her excitement validated the importance of my work. She no longer had a Chupa Chups in her mouth. She didn't take her eyes off the laptop screen, as if she were eagerly learning how to use the computer.

It's thrilling to have a client like Judith. I felt comforted when I thought of her. I ordered another beer and sucked it down in one gulp. I went up to my room, took a shower, and fell asleep.

The next morning, when I got to the Vienna Opera House, the woman from Hong Kong was already there. She had on dark sunglasses and was holding a Coke can.

"Where are you taking me?" she asked.

"The Art History Museum of Vienna."

"Sounds good."

She downed the rest of her Coke and followed me. If you walk to the west away from the Opera House, you hit the Art History Museum and the Natural History Museum. April in Vienna was still chilly, the wind strong and piercing. We had to hunch against the wind.

The Art History Museum housed the Hapsburgs' fine art collection. Facing it was the Natural History Museum, which used to be a palace. Standing in Maria-Theresa Square, looking at the majestic Renaissance architecture, we agreed that the art inside would be comparatively boring. But we decided to go into the warm building to get away from the gusty wind. We checked our coats and belongings and, feeling unburdened, walked down the corridor that aristocrats would have sauntered through ages ago.

Like we expected, the pieces on display were nothing exciting: mummies of Egyptian pharaohs, jackal statues guarding the mummies, castrated but grand limbless Greek warriors.

We lingered in front of a Kuros statue, excavated in the fifth century B.C.

"Isn't that amazing?" I asked.

She shook her head. "No. I hate dynamic statues."

We went up to the second floor, which displayed mostly post-Renaissance works. We wandered around casually as if we were looking at scenery. A special exhibit, Eroticism in Masterpieces, was in one corner of the gallery. We entered the room without much thought.

There were paintings by Titian, Rubens, and Caravaggio, with characters like Mars, Eros, Venus, and Zeus. I felt for the artists who couldn't depict love between real people and could only show eroticism through the prism of mythology. I wasn't turned on no matter how hard I tried to get in the mood. The eroticism in the paintings was too refined and cloistered to affect me. I pulled on her arm.

"Let's go."

She nodded. "I'm hungry."

We bought sandwiches at the museum café. I drank the water I had been carrying with me all day and she had a Coke. She looked more tired than she did the day before.

"Is it true that the night view of Hong Kong is amazing?" I asked.

"It's probably better than Hell."

We laughed.

"But that's a dumb question. Nobody thinks he lives in an amazing place," she countered.

She was right. I took another sip of Evian and lit a cigarette.

"Where are you headed after Vienna?" she asked.

"To the same place you're going."

"Where do you think I'm going?" Her eyes widened.

"Florence."

Since she came to Vienna from Berlin, I was certain she would go south. From here, Florence is the only southern city for which you can leave at night. If she were heading to Eastern Europe, she would have left from Berlin.

"How did you know?"

"People from Hell can read minds."

"I think Florence will be warm. Berlin and Vienna are too cold."

For someone from Hong Kong, even this weather would feel severely cold. That night she didn't go back to her pension.

The next night, in a train to Florence, we got a six-person compartment for just the two of us. She fell asleep as the train passed through the plains of Lombardy. I kept shifting around in my seat and gazed at her sleeping figure, instead of staring out the window.

The previous night, in Vienna, she'd fallen asleep like that. As soon as we had sex, she greedily gulped down some Coke from a plastic bottle. It seemed her thirst was unquenchable. She drank and drank until she could see the bottom of the bottle. When she was done, she fell asleep, as if she had finished all she had to do.

It's easy to have sex when you can't really communicate. I can focus on the sensations without thinking about anything else. She mumbled a few phrases in Cantonese and I was happy that I didn't have the need or the duty to understand. She probably felt the same way.

When the train arrived at the Italian border, customs officials and police officers boarded to check passports. Her passport had been issued in the name of Queen Elizabeth II. She looked for her Coke on waking, but her bottle was empty. She became flustered. I offered her my water bottle. She grimaced and refused it.

"No. I don't drink water."

True, I hadn't seen her drink water. She always drank Coke or some other soda.

"That's strange. Why won't you drink it? Don't they drink water in Hong Kong?" She glared at me. The hatred in her eyes was so piercing that I leaned back despite myself. "What?"

"Never offer water to me. I don't want to drink water. Ever!"

I was irritated, and also taken aback by her tone. The train crossed the border, stopped briefly in Padua, and continued on to Florence.

I fell asleep for a little while. When I woke up, it was still nighttime. The stars outside the window shone brilliantly. I cracked open the window. The noise of the wheels clattering on the tracks got louder. But she was sound asleep. The night air didn't feel chilly. Was it because we were getting closer to Florence?

At that moment, there was a loud bang accompanied by

screeching brakes and falling bags. She woke up. I stood up and stuck my head out of the window, but couldn't see anything. The conductor said something hurriedly in Italian and German over the PA system, but I couldn't understand it.

"Do you know German or Italian?" I asked.

"No."

We sat there, waiting for news. It seemed that either the train had collided with something or someone had activated the emergency brake. We sat in our empty compartment, blankly staring at each other. One hour went by, then another.

"Have you ever loved anyone?" she asked me.

"No."

"I have. When you work in a department store, a lot of men hit on you. We can't turn them down because we're in the service industry. We have to just smile and not get angry. I used to sell tea at the department store. This one guy bought tea every day, and talked to me. I never knew whether he wanted to buy tea or talk to me. Then one day he stopped coming. That was my first love. Because of that I don't drink tea."

"Did you sell water after that?"

She glared at me. "You're a fucking asshole."

I was shocked at those words. She knew how to swear in English. She grabbed my Evian bottle out of my hand and guzzled the water down, as if on a dare. I watched her, feeling nervous. She emptied the bottle, glared at me again, and went out to the corridor. I followed her with my eyes. She headed toward the bathroom, swaying, then collapsed in the middle of the corridor. People, who had been milling about outside, tired of the delay, rushed over to her. I ran out, pushed through the crowd, and held her. I tried to get her on her feet. She bent over and started to throw up. I didn't know what to do. I ran to our compartment for some tissues and a plastic bag.

It had been two hours since the train stopped. So she wasn't motion sick. What was it? She yanked the tissues and plastic bag out of my hands to clean up her vomit. She disappeared into the bathroom, snapping, "I told you not to give me water!"

"I won't in the future," I murmured, chastised.

The train started moving slowly while she was still in the bathroom. Another announcement was made in Italian and in German.

I caught myself thinking of Judith again. After mulling over several methods, she finally chose gas. I expressed my reservations: "That's a little dangerous."

"Dangerous? Ha!" She laughed. It was a little funny. I was warning of danger to someone dreaming of suicide.

"Gas sinks to the floor because it's heavier than air. It could leak downstairs or even explode if someone breaks down your door."

"An explosion would be interesting. But I don't want to go with so much fanfare. Isn't it your job to make it work?"

There was a way to do it. After a certain time, I could

call the police. She liked that idea. I explained the procedure.

"Around eleven P.M. you seal the door and windows so the gas doesn't leak out. Next, you unplug everything, including the phone. If something sparks it could blow everything up. Then go next door and ask them to keep an eye on your apartment because you're going out of town. So if someone comes by, they can tell him you're not here. Then you write a will. You could also write it in advance. If there's a will, the cops will quickly determine it a suicide. It's good to write a will in detail. The police are suspicious of vague wills. If a murderer wrote the will, it's usually vague. You should specifically mention people close to you. Like, so-and-so, I'm sorry for doing such and such. That will make things easier for me to deal with."

"That sounds hard."

"If it's too hard, you can choose something from examples I have, but I think it's good to write your own will since it's the last thing you'll ever write."

She sat down to write her will right away. She tore up a few drafts but diligently wrote away. I watched TV and drank whiskey.

We arrived in Florence, the city of flowers, around eleven in the morning. We were three hours late. As soon as we got off the train, we got her a Coke. She chugged it greedily. We walked leisurely over to the Duomo, the symbolic structure of Florence. In front of the majestic church, decorated in white and green marble, there was a baptistery made from the same marble. Carvings in relief by Renaissance sculptors like Ghiberti graced the doors on four sides of the masklike Duomo.

"I don't like towers," she said, glancing up at the bell tower of the Duomo.

"Why?"

"They make me sick."

We sat on the Duomo steps and smoked. She snuffed her half-smoked cigarette out and remarked, "When I love deeply, I vomit."

"You loved a tower?"

"Dumbass. Nobody loves towers. I want to see the Ponte Vecchio." She showed me a picture of the Ponte Vecchio in her guidebook. We passed the Galleria degli Uffizi and arrived at the bridge lined with disintegrating, generations-old shacks.

"I've wanted to see this bridge for a long time," she told me.

"How did you know about it?"

"I had a British Airways calendar, and January was the Ponte Vecchio. I liked those rickety houses. That picture had the sun setting over the bridge. Isn't the bridge beautiful?"

But the bridge wasn't that beautiful in real life. It looked like a shantytown about to be dismantled. It failed to hide the hardships it had gone through over the years.

"I like how everything is mixed together and mismatched. And it's warm here." Her voice was tinged with suppressed tears. It was true; Florence was much warmer than Vienna. We went to the flea market and a couple of art museums, then back to our small and shabby hotel. She showered and changed as soon as we entered our room. I drank a lukewarm beer I'd bought at the store.

"How do you have sex in Hell?" she asked, sipping beer.

"I don't have sex in Hell."

"Liar. I think the only thing you do is have sex."

"Why do you think the only thing I do is have sex?"

"Because you make me sick."

"Then why did you sleep with me?"

"You know when you feel like throwing everything up? My stomach is always filled with weird things. That's when I feel the urge to have sex."

"What did you do after you quit your job at the department store?"

"I worked at a bar."

"Were you a bartender?"

"No, I was too young. They wouldn't let me mix drinks."

"Then what did you do there?"

"I was a mannequin."

"A mannequin?" I thought of the movie *Mannequin*. It was about a man who loved a plastic model who turned into a person. Are humans that much better than mannequins? Why do cartoon monsters and cyborgs want so badly to become human?

"I was a mannequin sitting on the bar. I wasn't sitting at the bar, I sat on top of it."

"What were you doing up there?"

"I was wearing paper clothes."

"Huh, that's funny."

"The clothes were made of pieces so that you could take them off, one by one. And each piece had a price written on it. People would drink, look at me, then pay to take off a piece of paper corresponding to that price. I wasn't supposed to say anything. People always wanted to talk to me. They wanted to see how my expression changed whenever they took off a piece of paper."

"I would have wanted the same thing."

"Yeah, but I was too young to understand. You know, humans are really strange. I became very different when I was wearing that patchwork paper dress. I didn't like it when guys took off a piece of paper, leering, but then I would wish someone would take off all the pieces. I was sad when there still was paper stuck to my body after we closed. I was the sum of ragged scraps of paper, and I was sitting there, a mannequin with pieces of paper that couldn't be converted into money. Do you get that feeling? I doubt it. It's hard to understand a mannequin."

"Uh-huh."

"One day this guy came in. From that day on, he sat in front of me every night and drank. He didn't talk to me once. He drank a beer and took off a piece of paper from my left breast worth thirty Hong Kong dollars. He drank another beer, looking at my bare breast. He would do the same the next night, and the night after that. He was only an unimportant salaryman. He wore a wrinkled suit and a cheap tie. I wanted to give him my left breast. I wanted him to fondle it all night and suck it and fall asleep doing that. But I couldn't. If I got caught sleeping with a customer, my breast would be cut off. For a month, he came in, looked at my left breast, and went home. I thought I was going to go crazy."

She grabbed my beer and took a sip.

"Then one day another guy showed up. He was wearing an Armani suit and looked like a small-time gangster. As soon as he sat down in front of me, he took off the three-hundred-dollar piece, the most expensive one. He left all the other pieces. I actually felt less humiliated. He then took off all the other pieces, all the way down to the cheapest scrap. Then he beckoned, someone ran over, threw some clothes on me, and put me in a car. He was the first man who took all the pieces off. I thought I should love him."

She gulped Coke straight from the bottle.

"I started living with him. I wore a paper dress at home. Only for one person, for him. Each time, he paid and took off the scraps. Then I would work for him. But I never slept with him. Instead, during the three months I lived with him, I drank his sperm, probably more than a liter. He didn't ever try to screw me. After he took off all the paper clothes, he made me kneel and eat his cum, then fell asleep. Afterward, every time, I drank the water he had in his house—Evian. My mouth always smelled like his juice and later the Evian started tasting like it. I began to collect it. He thought it was funny. I told him I would save it and drink it later. Whenever he came, I would funnel it in an empty Evian bottle and keep it in the fridge. Finally, when the bottle was full, I put on the paper dress again. He paid for all the pieces. He sat in a chair and waited for me to kneel. I went behind him and put a gun to his head. I forced him to drink all the stuff in the Evian bottle. He threw up. I left him there and ran out. Then I came on this trip."

Her story smelled of fiction. But I couldn't tell where the lies ended. The last part might be a lie. Maybe that guy dumped her. She might have fantasized every night about threatening him with a gun and forcing him to drink his own ejaculate. But it didn't matter. Whether her story was true or somewhat false, it was clear that she vomited whenever she drank water—something must have happened to her to cause that kind of reaction.

"I guess we're both fugitives," I commiserated.

"What are you running from?"

"I'm not in such a desperate situation as you. I always run from myself. I have to do that in Hell."

"Try drinking your own sperm. Then you won't have to keep running away."

She smiled bitterly and climbed on my lap, facing me, and kissed me. A gap persisted between us, as vast and fundamental as the ability to drink water. Even though our lips were joined, even though we had sex, there was a river we could never cross.

After, we stumbled out of the chair. She reached for her Coke, but grabbed the Evian. In the dark, she might have thought the water was Coke. I left her alone. Keep vomiting, I thought. You'll stop when you can't anymore.

The next day we parted ways. I went to Brindisi to go to Greece and she left for Venice. Luckily, the train to Brindisi came first. She waved from the platform. I wonder if she went back to Hong Kong.

I return to the computer and reopen the file. I have to edit the last part of the novel. I hope I can finish before dawn. When I work at night, I'm disrupted only when the sun rises. I banish thoughts about Judith and the woman from Hong Kong and settle back to work.

PART IV
MIMI

"Boredom is no longer my love."

—Arthur Rimbaud, "Bad Blood"

WHEN C GOT THE PHONE CALL FROM K, he instinctively knew it was about Judith. C always got bad news early in the morning. In a subdued voice, K related that Judith had passed away peacefully. K didn't criticize him, which made C feel all the more uncomfortable. So he just listened. K didn't forget to ask before hanging up, "You did know it was her birthday the day you went away with her, right?"

"Yeah. I didn't believe her, though. I found out it was true after I got back."

"I didn't know it was her birthday until after she died." K hung up without waiting for C's reply. C looked at his watch. It was ten in the morning. He opened the curtains and sunlight filled the room. His head was empty. He went out to the balcony to smoke. He leaned on the railing and looked down. From the twentieth floor, it looked like the world was going about its business as usual. Nobody would be thinking about the woman resembling Judith this morning. He stubbed out his cigarette, went into the kitchen, and washed the dishes from the night before, piling them carefully on the dish rack.

The water was boiling on the stove. He made coffee and ate a piece of his day-old baguette. Hidden in the paper was an article about an exhibition opening that day. Only two lines were written about his work, so he skimmed the whole article before he finished eating. The article was merely a reprint of the publicity materials the gallery distributed to the papers, edited a little. He couldn't really trust the veracity of the other articles in the paper now that he knew this, so he glanced at the headlines and pushed the paper away.

C thought back to that snowy day. Judith, who had disappeared five months ago, riding away on the snowplow, seemed more and more real. He felt her absence infiltrating his life, though he hadn't thought about her in months. He burrowed into the sofa and tried to remember Judith. But he couldn't remember anything specific, not even her face. Instead, images of the North Pole, Chupa Chups, a snowball, and dull sex circled in his head.

The phone rang about five times before the answering machine picked up. He heard Mimi's voice as he was lathering his face with shaving cream.

"Are you there? I'm coming up now."

The razor nicked his chin. Blood turned the white foam pink. He kept shaving. He slapped on some Old Spice, whose bottle had a picture of a ship departing in search of spices. The cut stung. He went into his bedroom and put on some clothes, and the bell rang.

Instead of saying hello, Mimi pushed her nose into his cheek and sniffed. She nodded, about what he didn't know, and pulled off her tall boots. She sank into the sofa and hugged her knees to her chest.

"Coffee," she slowly whispered, as if imparting an important secret.

"I don't have any ground coffee... Would you like some lemon tea instead?"

She shook her head. "Grind some now, I'll wait."

C went into the kitchen to grind some coffee beans. She hummed while he transformed the beans into a fine powder. She often crooned tunes he couldn't place. He put the grounds in a strainer and made coffee while she kept humming, not budging from the sofa. C poured the coffee into a blue mug and handed it to her. Mimi didn't touch it. She just stared blankly at the balcony and beyond.

"Are we working today?" she asked, still gazing toward the balcony.

"Today?"

She nodded. "I want to work today." She stood up and started taking off her skirt.

He grabbed her wrist. "You don't have to take it off right now. Have some coffee first."

But she slipped off both her skirt and sweater. "Doesn't mean I have to have them on. Just get me a robe."

He brought her his robe, which was big on her. Only

after she shrugged into the robe did she pick up her mug and relax.

"Good coffee," she commented. Holding the mug in her right hand, she reached behind her head and unclipped the pin holding her hair in place. Her brown hair danced down her shoulders like it would fill the entire room, and he felt slightly dizzy. She shook her head a few times to smooth out her tousled hair. The scent of soap enveloped him, and he burned the roof of his mouth with coffee.

Three months before, C sat in a café on Daehak Street, early in the morning. Another café was across the alley, which was so narrow that two cars passed one another only by scraping their side-view mirrors. He was waiting for a friend to talk about an exhibit. The friend was an hour late. Even though C knew his friend was always late, he always went to meet him on time. He cherished the time he spent waiting for someone to show up. During that time, he wasn't obligated to do anything. He could read a book or people watch. This was the only time he didn't suffer from a sense of debt to himself. He was free from the compulsion to be productive. On the other hand, making someone wait is unpleasant. Being late makes you impatient and servile. That's why C was always the one waiting.

The big windows of the café provided a pleasant view. The café across the street did the same. C felt like he was looking at a mirror. He sat by the window, looking at the café across the street, where a man in a gray suit glanced at him, drinking coffee. Sometimes their eyes met, which made him feel uncomfortable. Each time he looked away, focusing instead on the people walking by. Some of them looked into the café, and their eyes met his on more than one occasion. The windows were like a screen. He was an actor drinking coffee and the people walking by were the audience. Or it could be the other way around: The pedestrians were the actors. Passerby 1, Passerby 2, Passerby 3 . . . Most walked without looking at him, performing their parts professionally, but a few looked into the camera like first-time extras. Each time that happened, he felt annoyed. C continued to wait for his friend, sometimes as a member of the audience, other times as the actor.

When that game got boring, he started envisioning the work he was going to show in the exhibit. He only had a vague concept: a piece that combined video and performance art. He didn't yet have a specific theme or a technique he wanted to employ. His ideas alternated between the grandiose, morphing into environmental art like Christo's draping of a Pacific island, and his reality, where he only had two camcorders and a Mac. He had gone back and forth between the Pacific Ocean and his apartment studio three times when a woman walked into the opposite café. He still remembers how the wind fanned up her long, straight hair and let it float back down again, like water from a fountain. He squinted, tracking her with his eyes. She sat down at the bar near the window facing him, her coffee on a tray. She was wearing a thin leather jacket and shorts, and he could make out her legs through the picture windows. He kept watching her.

She was different. It wasn't that she had a unique sense of style or that she had bad posture. He wondered what it was that made her so attractive. Only when his ignored cigarette dropped ash into his coffee cup did he figure out her secret. She was a perfect actress. She didn't look in his direction once. She just sipped her coffee in the sun, delicately. She didn't read or rifle through her purse or touch up her makeup. She looked like she was concentrating on projecting herself through the windows, the screen. Her only movement was to caress her hair that fell over her shoulder each time she lowered her head, then flip it back.

"Sorry, were you waiting long?" His friend appeared. C's eyes had started to sting because he was so engrossed in the voyeuristic game of watching the woman behind two windows. His friend was a curator at G gallery in Insadong, which was putting on this exhibit. The curator sat down and followed C's gaze across the street. C was unable to tear his eyes away.

"Why is she over there?" the curator clucked. He went across the street and escorted the woman to their table. It was surreal. He was shaken, the way he always feels when he sees a TV ad where a tiger leaps out of the screen. The woman was now sitting across from him, having walked through the screen and the lens of the camera. He was a little embarrassed.

The curator introduced them. "This is Yu Mimi. I assume you know who she is." The two nodded in greeting. C had heard of her. People had talked about her performance art at a few gatherings. But it never occurred to him that he would meet her like this, so he sat back quietly and let his friend talk.

"We invited her to perform on opening night because we want to open with a bang. We think it'll be a nice mix, because we're mostly exhibiting video and installation," the curator explained, glancing at C as if he were uncomfortable with the way C was staring at Mimi. She was pale up close. Smoky eye shadow contrasting with her pearly skin gave her a decadent beauty. She looked to be around thirty and somehow reminded him of Judith. Judith, who wasn't interested in anything, and Mimi, who seemed so confident and self-assured, didn't have anything in common on the surface. Was it her scent? Her posture? The way she looked at people? C couldn't figure it out.

The curator rambled on about the exhibit's purpose and significance, but Mimi looked bored. Her aloof demeanor effectively canceled out the grand aim of the exhibit, and the curator became flustered. At the end of his spiel, the curator asked whether she would do him the honor of performing on opening night. She looked like she would refuse, but she assented readily. The curator looked at C, surprised by her agreement. C felt like he had to say something to fill the silence.

"That's great. It's going to be a wonderful exhibit, thanks to you."

She only smiled a little. She asked, "What kind of work do you do?"

He hesitated, unsure of what he should say, and the curator answered for him.

"Oh, C? He studied Western art in college but now he does video and installation. Video art is really how he pays the bills." The curator looked at C as if for approval. C nodded imperceptibly.

"What will you be showing in the exhibit?" she asked.

He saw that her eyes, which had been languorous during the curator's monologue, were starting to sparkle.

"Well, it's still in the planning stages, so I'm not exactly sure what it'll be."

"Ah, I see," she said, assuming her original bored expression. She pursed her lips and sucked some kiwi juice she had ordered up through a straw. Closing his eyes, C imagined the green liquid going down her throat and spreading throughout her body. He could see her body turning green, the kiwi juice seeping into her capillaries. That image called to C's mind the seventeen-inch screen through which he watched the world. The screen in C's imagination fuzzily captured the image of Mimi drinking kiwi juice. The image of Mimi onscreen sharpened into focus and overlapped with the real Mimi. He opened his eyes. She was still sipping kiwi juice through a straw. He held his breath and suggested out of the blue, "Won't you work with me?"

She didn't seem surprised, but she stiffened a little. She shifted in her seat, flipping her hair behind her shoulder. "Pardon? I'm not sure I understand."

"I'd like to capture your performance onscreen. Like Nam June Paik's *TV Cello*. I would film you, edit and transform the work, and on opening night you could perform your piece, live. Behind you would be my work. A meeting of performance and video art. What do you think?"

His palms started to sweat. He jabbered on, trying hard to convince her to agree, even though he didn't really have a clearly formulated idea. An unstoppable urge to capture her on film propelled him. He recognized that he was dangerously attracted to her, but he couldn't resist. She quietly looked into his eyes.

"Know how to ride a bike?" she asked, breaking the long silence.

"Of course," he answered, surprised by the sudden turn in conversation.

"A lot of people said they'd teach me how to ride a bike. I don't know why they wanted to. I guess learning to ride a bike is hard to do on your own. They hold on to the bike from behind, but as soon as they let go, I wobble and fall over. Whenever someone offers to teach me how to ride a bike, I treat them skeptically."

C couldn't figure out why she was talking about a bike, but didn't interrupt.

"Just now, hearing you propose to film my performance, I thought of the people who wanted to teach me how to ride a bike. I don't really know why, yet. I haven't ever filmed or photographed my performances. For some reason, I get the feeling that this would be more dangerous than learning to ride a bike, maybe because it's something new?"

She paused, playing with her hair.

"Give it a shot. C is very talented," the curator piped in.

She smiled feebly. "It's a very strange day. One of those days where you can't refuse anything asked of you."

She took out a piece of paper from her purse, scribbled her number on it, and handed it to C.

"Call me. But I might change my mind." Leaving behind traces of her wispy silhouette, she exited the café.

"Isn't she hot?" the curator said, grinning. "There are two types of beauty, seductive and self-protective."

"Which do you think she is?" C asked.

"I'm not sure. I guess the only way to know for sure is to get close to her. It's weird. She's famous for not letting herself be photographed or filmed. Did you know that?"

"No." C shook his head.

"She never allowed it. So you can only see her performance in person. People who've seen it say it's amazing. It's possible that it's made to be something greater than it really is because her reputation was built on word of mouth. Anyway, be careful. A lot of people got screwed when they started hanging out with her."

Even before the curator's warning, an instinctive sense of precaution was growing inside C. He hadn't forgotten that the things he was attracted to were usually the very same ones that pushed him into an abyss. Mounted butter-flies were the first things that gripped his fascination. He was still captivated by his old fantasy where the butterflies came alive, flying around with pins rammed through their bodies.

But why did he push sharp pins through his most trea-sured possession? How did he do it at such a young age, when he wouldn't have been able to do it now? Had he been seduced by butterflies or the act of capture?

In any case, one spring day, all the butterflies burned to ash. The fire that burst forth from the kitchen devastated the entire house in a matter of seconds, and C, coming home from school, sobbed, mourning his butterflies. His mother tried to soothe him by telling him, C, *we can always build a new house*. C cried harder.

When K arrived at Judith's apartment, he found that every trace of her had been erased. Someone had already moved in. K sat in his Stella TX, parked in the lot in front of the building, and listlessly listened to the radio. The conversa-tion he had with his brother that morning had been unpleas-ant. C had reacted as nonchalantly as if he were hearing about an incident written in the newspaper. C had slept with Judith. Didn't that count for something? K couldn't under-stand his brother. A week ago Judith swallowed sleeping pills, turned on the gas, and committed suicide. It had been five months since he'd seen her, and she left like that, with-out contacting him.

What had happened between Judith and C? The only thing K knew was that C also had no idea that Se-yeon died.

K started the car. He smelled a faint acrid smell, like the engine oil burning, but didn't pay much attention. He didn't know where he was going even when he took a ticket from the Gungnae tollbooth on the Seoul-Busan Highway. As soon as K's taxi went through the tollbooth, it roared up to the speed limit and beyond. He weaved through the cars emerging from the tollbooths and went into the left lane, feeling his body being pulled back. Unlike other times, the sensation was foreign and made him feel lonely. He pressed his foot on the gas.

K inserted in the tape deck a cassette tape he'd bought a few days before from a street vendor and turned up the volume as high as it would go. The speakers screeched, the high notes warped. K opened all four windows. He couldn't think through the sound of the cars whizzing by and the distorted noise from his speakers. He sped to Busan and returned to Seoul, making the trip twice. His eyes became bloodshot. Though he tried to fall asleep on the shoulder a few times, sleep never came over him.

C's studio wasn't ready to film Mimi's performance. C hurriedly checked the lighting and set up his two camcorders. On the floor, he spread a large canvas that had been leaning against the wall, and then mixed paint. When the paint was ready, Mimi took off her robe, hung it up neatly, and walked over to the canvas, naked. The white canvas was blank. She studied the canvas and the camcorders. Then she squatted and examined the surface of the canvas. She smiled slightly, pleased with the rough texture.

White canvas. Someone once theorized that primitive man started to create art because of a fear hidden deeply within the human soul. The mere existence of a white blank wall is terrifying. That's why children scribble on walls and scratch the surface of new, shiny cars with knives. Frightened of an empty room without any furniture and paintings, people fill it up and refill it again. A late-night phone call, where you only hear the caller breathing, brings insomnia with its emptiness, its absence of conversation.

The theory that art originated from fear interested C when he first started to paint. It was a small but important consolation for him, who had to live off his art, that one could control inscrutable fear and transform it into art. But he still sometimes asked himself: *What am I really afraid of?*

C focused on Mimi and the canvas with his camera. Mimi circled the canvas as if she didn't trust it.

"Okay, let's start," he told her.

Mimi snapped her head toward him and asked, "Can I get a drink?"

She took three gulps straight from the whiskey bottle.

"Stop drinking," he ordered, grabbing the bottle out of her grasp, and held out the paint. Mimi kneeled and dunked her long hair into the paint. He started filming. She carefully soaked her hair in paint, slowly got up, and stepped onto the top left corner of the canvas. She started painting with her hair. As she painted, the paint got on her hands, knees, and blue paint took over the canvas. The cameras followed her movements from the front and the side. When she reached the middle of the canvas, propelled by her energetic head swishing, she raised her body. Her hair, drenched in blue, was disheveled, and the paint was dripping down her body. It trickled down between her breasts, down her spine, in between her buttocks. She solemnly rubbed her body, so that the paint would coat her skin. She became blue.

"Don't look into the camera," C called, his eye to the camera, but she ignored him and looked straight into the lens. Finally she rubbed her blue hands on her face. When she looked into the camera, a chill went down C's spine. He stepped back, overcome by a strange, inexplicable guilt.

"Let's take a break," C said, wiping sweat from his forehead.

She sighed, as if she had returned to herself, and stepped off the canvas.

"Do you want to wash up?"

She shook her head. She drank the leftover whiskey.

"You're different," she said, removing the bottle from her lips. Her body glowed, like a firefly in a dark cemetery. She continued, her face smudged in blue. "I've met a lot of guys. I've slept with them and sometimes lived with them. But they couldn't deal with me. I don't know why. So how can you handle me? What makes you different from them?"

She was starting to relax. It was less because of the

liquor and more because of the crazy spectacle she put on. He was envious of her for a second, an artist able to get drunk from her own work. He couldn't be immersed in himself like that, not when he was working.

It seemed an extraordinary indulgence in oneself.

Mimi came by C's apartment for the first time three days after their initial meeting at the café. They watched a video-tape of his work in his studio. She showed interest. Looking at her hungrily watching the tape, he realized that she looked like a character in a Boris Vallejo drawing. But he couldn't remember its title. He was in the habit of remembering images, not words.

"I like performance art. Or miming," Mimi said.

"Video art is also fascinating," he ventured cautiously.

She didn't agree. "All you do is look at something through a lens. You edit it, looking at a monitor, then show it on-screen. It's no longer real if it's filtered."

"I guess you could think of it like that. But isn't all art a filter for reality? Drawings or sculpture change reality in some way and make it more real. You could say art is a re-flection of reality."

C studied her expression. She didn't look like she was going to back down.

"Performance art is different. I meet things directly. I see death and lust in the audience's eyes. Depending on what I see in their eyes, my work changes immediately. If the purpose of art is to confront beauty, especially live beauty, aren't all other artistic forms fake? They are compromises and the residue of the desire for useless immortality. All criticism of performance art starts with the fear of true beauty. People preserve beauty because of their obsession with immortality. They are slaves of dead art." She was getting worked up.

"Immortality? What's wrong with immortality? Don't we all want to be immortal?"

She regarded him with disdain. "Fine. Let's stop arguing. But I don't want to force myself to make dead art. Life is short. There isn't enough time to do everything I want to do."

"Why are you afraid of the camera?"

She widened her eyes, insulted. "Afraid? I just don't like it."

"Fear often wears the clothing of hatred. If you are going to learn how to ride a bike, you have to turn the handles the direction you're falling, and pedal hard."

She mulled over his words for a long time, silent. But her silence wasn't a sign of being convinced. "Isn't it the same for you, too? You're scared of dealing with me face-to-face. Isn't that why you brought out the video? Isn't it? It could be you who need to turn the handles in the direction of the fall." Her voice got higher and higher, but lost confidence. He felt unsure.

"Well, then," he said, trying to breathe evenly. "Why did

you agree to work with me? Why did you come all the way to my studio?"

"I don't know." She retreated and lit a cigarette. "I don't quite understand it myself. I sometimes think my work wouldn't be mine anymore if I put it in another medium. Actually, if that ever happened, I feel like the life that I've been maintaining against all the odds would crumble at the foundation. It's stupid, I know. Other people would think it's no big deal. But I think I've taken it too far. I wonder if there's another way to make art."

"I see. Then let's try working together."

She assented. She blew out a long stream of smoke. Bluish smoke filled the room. Her eyes followed the smoke dissipating slowly.

"I slept with a guy for the first time when I was a senior in high school. He was my Korean teacher. He would call me out and take me to a nearby motel. He sometimes got me out of study periods and sometimes even called on Sundays. It wasn't rape or consensual sex, but something awkward, in between. You know what I mean, right? I don't think I was in love with him. It was a point of pride for me that he would take off his clothes in front of me, when he was so popular with the other girls.

"Then I met his wife. A woman I'd never seen before beckoned me out of my study period. I knew who she was immediately. She was icily confident. She said to me calmly, 'You're that girl. You're very pretty. Do you like your

teacher?' I nodded, but not because I liked him. I was acting like I did because I didn't like her coldness. Then she
said gently, as if to a younger sister, 'You can't do this. Especially with him. Okay?' What do you think I did then?"

"I don't know." C shrugged, wondering if she'd just
nodded passively.

"I screamed. I screamed and screamed like a deranged
psychopath, stomped my feet and screamed, until all the
students and teachers rushed out. I still can't forget her expression. She was calm, unmoved. What kind of person
does that? I was scared. So I kept screaming, and finally my
Korean teacher appeared. Then his wife slapped him and
walked away, dignified, across the playing field. Everyone
understood what that had been all about. The teacher
didn't come back to school, and we heard he got divorced.
Everyone blamed me for it. It's ridiculous, isn't it?"

Mimi cleaned up in the bathroom. She scrubbed her entire
body meticulously, as if she were going to immerse herself
in holy water for a religious ritual. She washed her hair with
solvent to get all the blue paint out.

"What color are we doing next?" she asked.

"How's black?"

She nodded and dunked her hair in the paint again, her
butt in the air, drenching her hair in paint as if she were
alone. During her performance, Mimi's hair became a writing instrument, its thickness and shine gone wayward. An
unsuppressed lust tore through C like a torpedo whenever

he looked at Mimi writhing. He tried to concentrate on the act of filming.

Her body morphed into the handle of a brush, her hair into bristles. C followed her movements through the bluish viewfinder. He was too used to looking at the world through a lens. He realized that when he walked around, he unconsciously blocked every scene as if he were looking through a frame, believing more in the images he edited on tape than things he saw in person. He actually became attached to the edited images. The video camera was his shield, a small but safe refuge from the vast unknown. This might be why he can't get closer to this seductive performance artist. For a split second, C wanted to stay in his world, the world he knew, one he'd reflected on, created, and captured. Mimi hummed some tune he didn't recognize. He thought she might be crying.

He wouldn't ever leap over this distance between them. He despaired, realizing he would never muster up the courage to cross the chasm separating him from the world, the *objets* he manipulated into art, and the women he'd been with. He thought about Judith, who had walked to the North Pole. When he turned thirty, he had realized that the ability to love another is a skill.

K's taxi was pressing beyond 170 to 180 kilometers per hour, whipping dangerously past Gumi on the two-lane Seoul-Busan Highway. A tunnel sped toward him and swallowed him up in a matter of seconds. The ringing in his ears became louder, but he didn't hear it. His senses were starting to slow down, to dull. Everything—the wind slapping his face, the shrieking music, his fatigue, his hunger, and speed—felt hazy and far away, as if he were dreaming. K's skill in avoiding a crash was more by instinct than rational judgment. When he emerged from the tunnel, the speakers blew, ripping the music away suddenly, leaving pure silence. His body lurched, unused to the quiet. His ears were ringing, pounding, pulsating as if something were stabbing him. The car swerved into the slow lane and skidded onto the shoulder. Instead of braking, he stepped lightly on the gas and recovered the car's balance. He managed to get back into his lane, only slightly scraping the guardrail in the process. Inexperienced drivers tend to brake in these situations, which causes them to flip over. It's crucial to make sure you handle the wheel lightly, quickly alternating between stepping on the accelerator and the brake to regain your bearings. When K had full control of the car, he slowed and pulled over. The only sound he could hear was the whoosh of passing cars. He felt like he was experiencing the kind of quiet that exists inside a womb. That silence bothered K. He got out of the car to get some air.

Where am I going?

K didn't have an answer. He stood next to his car, wondering where he should go, but he couldn't decide. He had never asked himself such a question. He'd always sat behind the wheel, stepped on the gas, and only then chosen a destination.

Mimi came to visit when C was almost done editing his film. She walked in the door, looking haggard. The woman who had thrashed passionately on canvas had disappeared without a trace. She seemed like a shell of her former self.

"How have you been?" he asked.

"I've been thinking about those people who believed their souls would be sucked out of them if they were photographed," Mimi joked, looking tired. She laughed awkwardly, the way people who haven't laughed for a long time do. A muscle twitched in her cheek.

"Come on in."

She did, slowly. She looked around, almost bewildered, as if she had never been there before, and sat on the sofa.

"Would you like some tea?"

"No, thanks." She shook her head. Her thick hair shimmered, following the movement of her head.

"What's up?"

"I was hoping I could see your tape of me."

"Sorry, no." He refused flat out.

"Why not? Why can't I see my work?" Her voice trembled, but she didn't beg. It was more of a monologue, like an actor's—something that was supposed to be internal, unheard by others, but actually needed to be spoken and heard to make sense.

"The tape has captured your work, but it's not really you. It's also me but not me at the same time, since it's my work, something I filmed and edited." He refused her request even though he didn't have a real reason for doing it. Cruelty breeds a secret pleasure.

"That's not a good enough reason. I think I have a right to see it, at least once."

"Why do you want to see it?"

"I don't want to tell you. Please just let me see it." Mimi's words were hollow, dispersing into the air, again like a monologue.

C changed his mind. He decided to show her the tape. He found it and inserted it in the VCR. Mimi gnawed on her nails while it was being rewound.

"You bite your nails?"

She put her hands away, taken by surprise. "It's an old habit. I haven't done it in a long time. I guess I'm nervous."

Her nervousness was well founded. Her crazy abandon radiated from the video uncensored, passion exploding onto the canvas. Watching herself on the tape, she may have been facing herself for the first time.

C turned on the original, preedited tape. Mimi stared at the screen like a statue. A stillness enveloped the living room, as if a holy ritual were being performed. That mood even infected C, who had seen the tape many times, and he remained quiet, respectful. In the tape, Mimi was attacking the canvas with her whole body, slashing at the surface with black paint. Her hair slid over the smudged imprints left from her breasts, and her body slithered over it all, obliterating the strokes of paint. Throughout her performance, she mumbled incoherently, as if she were a Native American shaman casting a spell.

"Stop it," she ordered. C paused the video. She got up and paced the living room, muttering like she had in the video. A song, or maybe a spell. Her gaze never left the screen.

"You have to give this to me. You can't show that."

"What?" C got up, mirroring her panic. "You can't take it."

"Why? Why not?" She calmed down. He went over to her and pressed her shoulders down to get her to sit. She refused to look him in the eye.

"You can't throw away all the work we did," he insisted. The time you invest was proportional to the magnitude of your obsession. Nothing was free from this rule, be it love or art. "Why are you so afraid? That isn't you. It's been processed. Your performance has a value of its own, and video art is something completely different. It doesn't take away from your creation. Why can't you understand that?"

"Then why are you so afraid of me?" Mimi retorted, looking him straight in the eyes. A faint smile lingered on her lips.

He hesitated.

"Fine. I didn't think you'd give me that tape. You lust after the woman in the tape, instead of the real me. Because it's safer that way—you can't get hurt. You're right, Mimi in that tape isn't really me. It's you." Mimi walked out.

C blankly watched her leave. He couldn't move. He was paralyzed. Mimi was gone.

C was sick for three days straight. Weakness ravaged his body. He spent the entire time drinking beer and rewinding the tape and watching it over and over again.

When he recovered, he worked tirelessly to finish the project. He interlaced Mimi's performance with a possessed shaman's flailing motions he had filmed in Uijeongbu and with Ungno Lee's abstract letter art. Nobody called him, other than the gallery pressing him to submit his work. From time to time he called Judith, but she never picked up. A recorded voice told him it was the wrong number. He called other women he had dated a long time ago. They all answered his calls in flat voices. He had become a dangerous and bothersome existence to them.

He hadn't heard from Mimi by the opening night of the exhibit. He delivered his work and stopped by the gallery a few times to help with the preparations. He casually asked his curator friend about Mimi's whereabouts, but he didn't know either. *I don't think she's going to come, she's not answering the phone.* The curator shrugged and held his palms out, telling C he couldn't do anything about it. On those days, C went home and watched Mimi perform on tape all night.

At Singal Interchange, K merged onto Yeongdong Highway. Ten minutes later he got off the exit for Yongin Natural Park. Five minutes of navigating curves brought him to the

Yongin Racetrack. He pulled up to the parking lot, assaulted by a sharp pang of hunger. He bought a burger from a nearby fast-food stand and inhaled it. He sat by, watching the cars loop around the racetrack. All the cars were painted in flashy colors. Tobacco company logos, like Marlboro and Salem, were splashed on the entire length of the tricked-out cars. Most of the cars didn't have mufflers, making a loud roar even when they weren't running at their maximum speeds.

For the previous five years, K had revered velocity as his god. But his god wasn't generous. His god only appeared to those who sacrificed enough. Those few driving around this track were handpicked by this god. They spent hundreds of millions of won to refit their cars and to order custom-made tires. If they could do something to gain even one second during a race, they didn't hesitate to do it, using tricks like removing their backseats. These cars didn't have even an ounce of machinery or parts that were unnecessary for speed. K inherently understood their obsession.

The garage where K used to work was closed on Sundays, and he would head over here in a customer's car and spend the day like this, watching the cars zoom by, munching on a stale burger. Sometimes he would catch not a practice run but a real race. He would feel a sharp stab of excitement whenever cars flipped over. He was indescribably envious of the injured drivers crawling out from under overturned cars.

During a race, the cars hurtling past the others on curves

hardly ever used their brakes. The only way to get ahead was by using the gears and handling the car fluidly. The smell of burned rubber emanated from the track. If a driver missed shifting gears by a mere second, his car would flip over like a toy or skid off the track and crash. The race-car drivers knew this possibility better than K. Even though they knew it was that much more dangerous to go even a little faster, they gunned the gas without noticing they were doing it. These were the kinds of offerings the god of speed wanted. When one car was offered to the god of speed and crashed, the other drivers were relieved, not nervous. No doubt, they believed that another driver's misfortune lowered the probability that they would get into an accident. K would have thought the same thing.

But the god of speed didn't give K even the opportunity to be in an accident. He didn't hand K a Ferrari or a Lamborghini, cars that can easily surpass 250 kilometers per hour. He didn't even give him a car well tuned enough to enter a race. K got into the business of driving a taxi when he was faced with this reality. He stopped coming to the track. For a while he was satisfied with his Stella TX taxi. That's also when he met Se-yeon. But now she was no longer a part of this world.

I'm going to burn everything, K thought, picturing the photos of cars that filled a drawer in his bedroom. *They're all useless. My knowledge of a car's piston displacement, maximum speed, and horsepower doesn't make any differ-*

ence at all. K went back to the parking lot and climbed into his taxi. *No matter what,* he thought, *I have to see C.*

All of the participating artists were already gathered for a simple reception on the opening night of the exhibit when Mimi appeared at the entrance of the gallery. She was wearing a long, black coat that came down to her ankles and a black shawl. Ornate earrings dangled from her ears. Everyone hushed. She nodded politely to the crowd.

The curator made opening remarks, then Mimi walked in front of C's work and turned toward the audience. Standing under the spotlights and surrounded by the swelling music, she surveyed the audience like a queen and disappeared into a room off to the side. The lights dimmed. Everyone heard the door open. She was coming back out. When the sound of her footsteps stopped, the lights turned back on. The light bounced off her pale body in multiple directions. Behind her, in C's video, Mimi was writhing on the canvas, her entire being soaked in blue paint. She turned her head to glance at his work. Then she faced the audience again. A silver knife flashed in her right hand as she stepped onto the canvas. She slowly crawled up to the top of the canvas like a cat, raised her right hand high, as if she were startled by something, and slashed at the canvas. The noise of ripping canvas reverberated in the room. Heavy silence emanated from the audience. The white light beaming down on her revealed her as an *objet* on the white canvas.

Was she performing a sword dance? Her movements were infinitely slow but sometimes unpredictably nimble, like the dance of a raptorlike bird. Soon, the canvas was shredded, ragged, but she concentrated on slashing the canvas even more, her body undulating.

When there was nothing left to destroy, she stood up. Standing tall on the mangled canvas, like a statue of a goddess, she grabbed hold of her thick, silky hair with her left hand. With the knife she started to hack at her hair. Black clumps piled up on the white shreds of canvas. A chill spread up from the tips of C's toes. He shivered. He looked beyond Mimi to his work. In it, Mimi was thrashing about, her hair a pretty hue. His legs shook. The real Mimi was reaching the finale of her seemingly endless haircutting. When her hair was reduced into mere spikes, she dropped the knife. She stumbled into the room where she had left her clothes. C saw Judith in Mimi's silhouette. He thought of Judith, who had disappeared into the snow on her birthday, as he looked at Mimi walking to the North Pole. Cautious applause rippled through the audience. He couldn't stand there for another second.

He wobbled out of the gallery and walked around Insadong. He thought he should go into a teahouse and drink some warm green tea. He heard Mimi's voice behind him.

"I turned the handlebar in the direction I was falling. Now if I pedal hard, I'll probably be able to go away, somewhere else." She was wearing a black hat. "But you didn't."

He turned to look at her. The cars driving on the one-way road brushed past them, their headlights flashing intermittently.

"Do you know that we're the same breed?" she asked.

"You think so?"

"Do you want to know why I decided to work with you, when I've never allowed myself to be photographed?"

"Please."

"Last winter I performed at a party for the opening of a poet's café. It wasn't a big deal. It was similar to stuff I had been doing, and I performed it like I always did. Then I drank with a couple of people. It was cold and windy when I left. I walked, going past three bus stops. I don't know why. I just kept walking. This guy suddenly came up to me and asked me if I liked Gustav Klimt. I told him I did. He was a weird guy. I spent two days with him and decided to kill myself. I went against his recommendations and chose to cut my wrists in the bathtub. There wasn't a particular reason for it. You'd think that people kill themselves for some grand reason, but that's not true. Maybe it was because of that day's performance. For ten years, I had thought I was creating true art, but that day I didn't think I was. I got the feeling that I had never scrutinized myself. My whole life, I had felt like I was on the run. I was running away from all sorts of things, even though I kept thinking, this isn't it or this place isn't right. I told that guy everything. He held me without saying a word, listening to me talk. It was so cozy and warm that I must have smelled death. I finally realized what I was running away from."

She leaned against a building and continued, her gaze fixed on a placard hanging above.

"I saw myself in the bathroom mirror after I filled the tub and took off my clothes. I don't know why, but I didn't recognize myself. I sat in the tub, holding the knife he had given me, but I wanted to see myself in the mirror one more time. So I did. I repeated that three times. The guy smiled at me gently in the doorway of the bathroom. He told me, *I told you it wasn't going to be easy. Come on out and dry yourself. Give me the knife.* I gave him the knife and drained the tub. I dried myself off. As I was coming out of the bathroom, I suddenly got dizzy and fainted. I was in his arms when I woke up. He was wide awake. I felt like I had been reborn. That's when he told me, *It's not too late to come to me later. You should just rest now.* He said I needed rest. That I should think about this time as my last chance, and if there was something I had always refused to do, I should give it a try. I told him everything. That I wanted to see my work with my own eyes. That's when he gave me your name. When your curator friend approached me about this exhibition, I was happy to see your name on the participants' list."

"Then why did you want the tape back?"

"I don't know. I was afraid that I could be copied infinitely. And I couldn't stand that you had it, of all people. You should have slept with me. That would have been easier for both of us."

Mimi stared at him for a long time, quietly, then brushed past him. He didn't look back. He went back to the gallery. At the entrance, he saw a very familiar man, but he couldn't place him. The man nodded to C in greeting and C did the same. But he couldn't remember who he was. C walked past the man toward his work. A man was standing there, immersed in his work, someone C knew.

"What are you doing here?" C asked.

"I needed to say something to you," K replied, his eyes still focused on C's work.

"About Se-yeon?"

"I'm not here to say that it was your fault. I just want to tell you my side of the story."

"Yeah, these things aren't anyone's fault."

"I wasn't mad when I started smelling your lotion on Se-yeon. I didn't have a hard time accepting it or anything. It was just a bit tiresome." K's eyes were bloodshot. The vein near his temple was defined, protruding. C thought his brother looked like a hyperrealist drawing.

"But now that I'm looking at your work, I feel sick," K continued. "I feel nauseated at myself looking at it and at you who made it. I don't know if you'd understand. It doesn't matter if someone like Se-yeon is around or not. You're always going to live like the world is revolving around you, and I'm going to continue to live off engine oil. All I want to know is when my three-*kkeut* life is going to be over. I'm thinking of driving as fast as I possibly can today. I've always taken my foot off the gas at the last moment. But now I want to step on it to the end, until I really start flying."

"I can't stop you if you really want to do that."

"I knew you were going to say that. Oh, I came by to tell you something important. Do you remember when our house burned down?"

"Of course I do," C replied.

"All of your butterflies burned up and you cried all night. I was at home when it happened, but when you got home from school the first thing you asked about was the butterflies."

I probably did, C thought, and smiled bitterly.

"That day, I got home early from school. I took one of your butterflies and set it on fire. I wasn't thinking when the fire ate through the wings and slowly burned up the body. It was thrilling, exciting—if I think about it now it was the exact feeling I got when I got laid for the first time. Probably because I knew it was something you cherished. While I was burning up one butterfly after another, something caught on fire somewhere in the room. I didn't realize the blankets were on fire. So I kept lighting up the butterflies. Soon the fire burned the wall and spread to the ceiling, and I ran out of the house. When you came back and cried for the butterflies, I was scared and nervous but also ecstatic."

"Why are you telling me this now?"

"It's always bothered me."

"Don't worry about it. They're dead butterflies anyway."

"It's the same with Se-yeon," K said, and left the gallery. C didn't stop him, though it bothered C that letting K go like that came so naturally to him.

When C got back to his apartment, he turned on Mimi's performance tape. Like she had pointed out, now C could play her hundreds or thousands of times.

He watched until late at night. He grew sleepy. Immense fatigue clogged up the space between him and the screen. He dozed off for a while, but when he woke up to get some water, his eye caught the seventeen-inch screen, emitting light in the dark room, the electron gun inside the picture tube shooting irregular scanning lines. His apartment at that moment was a deep, dark cave, and the lonely blue monitor shining within was Mimi and at the same time Judith.

He pressed the rewind button. He was parched.

PART V
THE DEATH OF SARDANAPALE

POETRY

THE DEATH OF SARDANAPALE

I FINISHED EDITING THE NOVEL. IT'S

still dark. I insert paper in the printer tray and print out the manuscript. Maria Callas sings from the CD player the entire night. I like her. She was eccentric and did whatever she felt like doing. Her powerful voice once blew speakers that couldn't withstand its strength, but her voice is so wondrous that she can be forgiven for that.

I pick up an art book while the printer whirs. My dream is to fill my study with art books. I think I will be able to fulfill that dream when I'm done with this novel. The book I grab is about Delacroix. I'm not too fond of Romanticism, because sentiments are often too exaggerated. But I do like one Delacroix painting, *The Death of Sardanapale*. It's a scene of warriors acting under the Babylonian king's orders to kill the queen and concubines of the king, who is facing the fall of his kingdom. One robust warrior, with a cold expression, is grasping a naked woman from behind. She is leaning back. The warrior is stabbing her with a knife. The five-meter-by-four-meter canvas is bursting with a murderous energy. On the left side of the painting, there is a black soldier dragging the king's cherished horse to his death.

But it's not as if I like this painting because of its ornate Romantic style. In the top left corner, there is a man overlooking the carnage. This is Sardanapale, the Babylonian king. He's propping himself up on one arm and staring at the blood spurting out of his concubines and horse. He's the last thing you discover in this painting, because he's drawn in dark colors and is relegated to a corner of the canvas. In comparison, the scenes of murder are in bright, vibrant colors, and the women being slaughtered are blindingly nude. At the end, when you finally see King Sardanapale, you can't help but draw your breath and hold it. The finest part of the painting is the contrast between the king, coolly observing his downfall, and the dying, writhing women. Sardanapale, watching the bloody, frenzied ball, is really a portrait of Delacroix. He wanted to be a god. But I truly empathize not with Delacroix but with Sardanapale, the unfortunate king hosting a banquet of death amid the destruction of Babylon.

If a lesser artist had painted the same scene, he would have depicted Sardanapale with his arms over his head, grieving. But Delacroix understood the inner thoughts of a person presiding over death.

I decided to water the plants in the living room, which I haven't done in a long time. The flowers, filling the room, always looked the same. My flowers neither bloom anew nor fade. They don't break off, bleeding like the camellias of Seonun Buddhist Temple. I water my fake flowers once a week. I bought them when I moved to this place. I'm planning to throw them all out and bring in new floral arrangements next month.

Mimi, the only client who ever came to my apartment, was taken aback by the flowers blooming in my living room. When she realized they were fake, she refused to go near them.

"Why do you have so many of these fake flowers?"

"It doesn't matter whether they're fake or real, they exist only for you to look at them."

Mimi came back. But this time she looked brighter and happier.

"Did you see him?" I asked.

Mimi nodded. "It was a great project. But he can't save me."

"Nobody can save anyone," I replied.

Before settling into the bathtub, Mimi turned on Leonard Cohen's "Everybody Knows" and danced to it for a long time. Leonard Cohen's rough voice and the deep bass chords suited her dancing. I could hear the water running in the bathroom. The tub must have been overflowing. She listened to "Everybody Knows" about ten times, then went to the tub. Standing at the doorway of the bathroom, I watched her slowly lower herself into the tub, the water flowing over the rim. She glanced at me as she picked up the knife.

"Good-bye. Thank you for everything. I hope your flowers will bloom forever."

"Good-bye."

Her crimson blood, emerging from the depths of the tub, quickly stained the water. She struggled to keep looking at me in spite of her fading consciousness. Her eyes slowly drifted shut. This was a good time for me to leave.

"I'm going now. Have a good trip," I told her.

I took off my gloves when I left her apartment. I always wear gloves when I go to a client's place, to make sure my fingerprints aren't discovered. Sometimes there are clients who want sex, but I usually refuse. But if I can't, I use contraception. Not only do I have to be prepared for a possible autopsy, it's also indecent for a new life to awaken in a dead body.

Mimi left with flair. Judith went peacefully. I miss them immensely. Their stories are done, and my novel will be a beautiful fake-flower arrangement that will be placed on their graves. Everyone who reads this will meet me at one point, in Marronniers Park like Judith or in a deserted street like Mimi. I will approach them without warning and ask, "Nothing's changed although you've come a long way, right?" Or, "Wouldn't you like to rest?" When that happens, hold my hand and follow me. Don't look back, even if you don't have the guts to go through with it. Keep going, even if it's painful and wearisome. I don't want too many clients. And now, more than anything, I want to rest. My life is always the same and endlessly wearying, just like these bunches of fake flowers lining my living room.

After I submit this novel, I'm going to leave for Babylon. Will there be someone like Mimi or Judith waiting for me there, like that woman was in Vienna? Why does nothing change, even when you set out for a faraway place?

Printed in the USA
CPSIA information can be obtained
at www.ICGtesting.com
LVHW031234290524
781374LV00007B/69

9 780156 030809